NO HEROES

ANNA SEIDL

Translated by Siobhán Parkinson

Little
Island

NO HEROES

NO HEROES

First published in English in 2016 by
Little Island Books
7 Kenilworth Park
Dublin 6W
Ireland

Originally published in 2014
by Verlag Friedrich Oetinger GmbH, Hamburg, Germany
under the title *Es wird keine Helden geben*

ISBN: 978-1-910411-32-2

A British Library Cataloguing in Publication record for this book is available from the British Library
Cover illustration and design by Mick Minogue
Insides designed and typeset by redrattledesign.com

Printed in Poland by Drukarnia Skleniarz
Little Island receives financial assistance from The Arts Council/An Chomhairle Ealaíon and the Arts Council of Northern Ireland.
The translation of this work was supported by a grant from the Goethe-Institut, which is funded by the German Ministry of Foreign Affairs. Little Island is also grateful for the support of Ireland Literature Exchange.

10 9 8 7 6 5 4 3 2 1

For my parents
because you always believed in me
even when I didn't

It all starts with me sleeping in. If my boyfriend hadn't texted me, I'd have been late for school. But as it turns out, I made it to school on time. Which is how come I was there when it happened.

I wish now that I'd been anywhere else, as far away as humanly possible. And to think I used to be of the opinion that Latin homework was the worst thing in the world!

Then everything changed.

But the thing is, you can't know it all before it happens. It's not like a movie, where you know what's going to happen because you've seen the trailer. And there are no heroes either, because in the real world, everyone just thinks of themselves. You don't even think, what if …? Because it all just happens. And you can't do a thing about it, can you?

Could it be a fair punishment for what we've done? Everything – the whole day, the past week, the past year, my whole life – it all starts playing again in my head. I kind of wonder if my whole life has been one big lie.

Fear is my constant companion now, loneliness my best friend. That's why I'm going to tell you the story. Because I want to make something clear to you. I want you to understand.

CHAPTER 1

You can smell fear. You can get hold of it. But nobody dares to touch it. We all hold our breath.

It's under us. We can hear the shots. They're loud. Way too loud for my world of school and fun. And I don't know who it is. My best friend Joanne and I had just been told to go down to the ground floor by the teacher, and suddenly everyone is running. And then: *boom*. And again: *boom*.

Of course I know what gunshot sounds like. I am just as addicted to watching telly as the rest of the school. But it's different in real life. It's the same sound, only ten thousand times louder.

First, we just stop, Joanne and I. Then we start running too. Everyone upstairs is running. The teachers, the caretaker, the students. I can see Philip Schwarz, who is a year ahead of me. I used to fancy him a bit a few years back. He made an impression on me, always so perfect. I can see Lisa Schmidt too. I don't know anything about her. They're running as well.

I see all this, but I don't take it in. Nobody has really

taken anything in. How could we? We're just kids, after all, whether we're thirteen or thirty years old. Because we've never experienced anything like this. I'll tell you a secret. My first thought was just, *Shit, I have to get out of here.* I thought only of myself. Not of my teachers or schoolmates. Not even of Joanne. My first thought was for myself. And to be honest, I know it was exactly the same for everyone else. There are no heroes here. Because it's not a movie. It's reality, pure and simple. Joanne, Philip and I hide in the boys' toilet. Philip doesn't seem all that great now. He's just a bundle of nerves, cowering on the floor, breathing rapidly.

Joanne and I are bundles of nerves too. My hands are wet with sweat. My whole body is shaking. And there is pure fear strangling me, bearing down on my heart as if to stop it beating. That's how I know it's real. I'm not ready to die. I'm only fifteen, I've only had my first boyfriend for five months, I'm only in ninth grade. There are so many things that I want to do. And dying is not one of them!

Another shot sends me reeling. A thud on the floor, a shout, footsteps. He's getting closer.

It's weird. You'd think he'd be running, in a hurry. But it's not like that. You can hear his shoes, soft and rhythmic on the floor. Almost as if he were on his way to the gym, not shooting open the gates of heaven for terrified people. Or the gates of hell. Or the gates of nothingness.

Maybe you can imagine what it's like to cower on the cold floor of a stinking toilet. Maybe you can feel the way the cold grips your body, making it shiver uncontrollably. Maybe you can hear the silence, the deathly silence, when everyone just holds their breath and hopes it's someone else who gets it and that they themselves are safe. Maybe you really can. Or maybe not.

I thought I could. But I was wrong. Unfortunately, I was going to find out how things really are. I used to think you couldn't smell fear.

'Miriam,' Joanne whispers. Just my name. She gestures towards one of the cubicles with her head. She wants us to hide in there. The footsteps are getting louder. He's quite close.

I surprise myself by nodding. I didn't think I was capable of nodding. I touch Philip's arm, but his whole body is shuddering and he shakes my hand off. Joanne and I stare at each other for a moment.

Her eyes reflect my feelings: shock, incomprehension, fear. And I realise it is not going to end well. Not for all of us. That he's already shot that gun at some people, maybe killed them. And that he's going to do that to more people.

My eyes fill with tears of panic. I dig my fingernail as hard as I can into my arm, but the pain is nothing. It's more a relief, because it chases away the bad thoughts, even if only for a moment.

A strange noise startles me and Joanne. Philip is crying, screeching. Horrified, we gesture to him to shut up. But it's too late. The footsteps start towards our door.

We don't hesitate. Believe me, you wouldn't either. Quickly and noiselessly, we run into a cubicle. We climb up on the loo and then hunker down so that he can't see any bit of us. Or so I hope anyway. Then we angle the door like all the other doors. And we stop breathing.

Yes, we just leave Philip behind. And yes, I know the consequences. I know this could mean death for him. Heartless as it may seem – if I stayed, I'd be writing my own death sentence. Everyone thinks of themselves first here. There are no heroes. Heroes are an invention of the film industry.

The seconds seem to stretch. Coward that I am, I close my eyes, tightly, even though it doesn't make anything any better. Joanne grabs my hand and squeezes it so hard that the bones shift. I'm listening to the steps. They are getting louder, coming nearer. When the door is kicked open, we huddle together. Philip is still lying on the floor. We can't see him now. But we can hear him. He seems not even to notice that we've gone. He seems not to notice anything.

Time is dragging. I'd never have believed that a second could seem like an eternity. Then the shot comes. A roar. The smell of gunshot in the air. Like fireworks on New Year's Eve. Only different. More intense, more biting. Joanne and I are shaking. But neither of us makes a sound.

First survive, then grieve.

Another shot. Not a squeak out of us. Silence. And then a snuffle. The sound of the murderer running up and down. He's crying. Crying! As if *he* were a victim!

We are still holding our breath. He could still find us. And I don't want to end up like Philip. Lying on the floor with schoolmates behind me who daren't make a sound.

He leaves. I can hardly believe it. I was about to kiss life goodbye, but he's gone. Disappeared. Maybe we'll get out of this. Alive.

We wait for a bit. Maybe a minute. Hard to say. I've lost my sense of time. Now I pull away from Joanne and realise that I have absolutely no feeling in my right hand. Joanne has made some impression on my hand. I move it carefully. Then I move my feet. Joanne opens the door of the cubicle very softly.

And there he lies. White in the face. In a pool of his own blood. His brown hair looks lank. His eyes glassy. His mouth too pale.

I read in a book that dead people look peaceful. You would think they were only asleep. Philip looks like what he actually is: violently murdered, victim of a psycho.

I feel sick. Tears prick my eyes. But they don't flow. I'm too numb for that. Too shocked. Almost like a dead person myself.

Beside me, Joanne is sobbing softly. I put my hand over her mouth. I can feel her spittle on my palm. I take her in my arms and rock her gently back and forth, the way you rock a baby to sleep. The only thing that crosses my lips is a single little shush. It echoes around the tiled walls of the room and seems way too loud. When silence saves your life you redefine what's loud and what's soft.

I sit on the floor, hugging Joanne. What else could I do? I lay my head back and pretend I'm in a forest. The trees are rustling and I can hear the animals. Everything is the way it should be.

That calms me down a bit.

Until the next shot. That startles the hell out of me. It was just outside in the corridor and it echoes through all the walls.

It would probably have been smarter to stay sitting there. But I get up and go softly to the door. Joanne doesn't follow. She lies collapsed on the floor. Like a dead person.

I open the loo door just a crack. Then, very slowly, not sure what's awaiting me, I stick my head out. And what I see is a thousand times worse than anything else I have seen this day.

Because there is a boy lying on the floor out there, and it's Toby. My boyfriend. The sweet boy who texted me this morning so I wouldn't over-sleep because it's Monday. Toby is the boy I had my first time with, who was the first to say to me, *I love you.*

Toby is lying there on the floor. Toby, who wanted to win a teddy-bear for me at the funfair shooting gallery, but who brought me a sheep instead, because he didn't have enough points for the teddy. Toby, who'd made me breakfast every second Saturday when we'd spent the night in his parents' mobile home. Toby, who wanted to make me a pizza for our first date, only we both ended up being covered in flour. Toby, who only has to take my hand to comfort me. Toby, who only has to smile at me to make me feel beautiful and invincible.

This is the Toby who is lying there on the floor. *My* Toby.

He sees me. Even though he's lying about ten metres away. Begging me to help him.

And you can guess what's coming, right? You can see the scene playing out in front of you. I, Miriam Brand, hurl myself at him, distract the boy with the weapon in order to save my boyfriend. You watch as I courageously risk my life for him. Do everything for love of this boy.

Why should I lie? I stay where I am. I can't bear to look Toby in the eye. I turn my face away. I can't watch my boyfriend die. I can't listen to his loud, panicky wheezing, while at the same time his breath gets weaker and more irregular. I can't save him. Neither can I close the door again and sit down beside Joanne. I can't do anything any more.

Boom. Paralysed, I hear the next shot. I see two girls running along the corridor. Another shot. I witness the fall of a body. The body of a child who is only in fifth grade. Can hear her friend shouting. She flees. Runs into the nearest classroom, bangs the door shut. The gunman goes on down the corridor, is about fifteen metres from me.

And then, just like that, Joanne calls my name.

The gunman swings around …

… and looks me right in the eye.

CHAPTER 2

It only lasts a second. Only a second until he shoots. But I'll tell you what went through my head in this one second.

For the first time I'm seeing him face on. And I know him, this gunman who is on the rampage. It is Mathias Staudt. He's in 9C, a different class but the same year as me.

You know, it doesn't shock me that I recognise the shooter. What shocks me is that it is Mathias Staudt. Because Mathias had friends. OK, so he was pretty low down in the pecking order, but he had two very good friends in 9C. Or so I thought anyway. I never took much notice of him.

Mathias was just … not interesting to me. He's a bit of a mummy's boy. And he's not really very good looking. He's pretty small and a bit overweight and has too many pimples on his face. So I paid no attention to him, either as a friend or as a guy.

I know he fancies me. He even plucked up the courage once to ask me out. He wanted to go to some boring dancing-class end-of-year ball. Naturally, I just laughed at him. I know Toby and a few of his mates taunted Mathias Staudt. They hid his clothes in PE and they wrote *Mathias the Pig* or something on the board.

And now, here I am at the end of my life. Suddenly I feel a cold wind blowing around me. A couple of windows are open and the rain is coming in. I realise that a girl from eleventh grade is hiding under the window-seat. She looks at me fearfully. I don't react. I feel a thousand years older than her.

I can feel my whole body again, even the hand that Joanne clutched so tightly. Only now do I realise how much it hurts. And only now do I notice that my left arm, where I dug my nails in earlier, is bleeding and throbbing.

It's as if I'm only waking up properly, now that I'm at the end of my life.

I'm sorry I didn't hug my dad this morning. It would only have taken five seconds. I'm sorry I didn't ring my grandma back yesterday. I regret not having told my mother how much I hate her for having left me and Dad. I should have made a snow angel last winter, no matter if it's childish. I'm never going to be able to do it now, and this realisation bloody well hurts.

I'm never going to celebrate my sixteenth birthday as planned. I'm never going to get married. Never going to sit on the terrace as an old woman with my equally old husband at my side, surrounded by our grandchildren.

Images pass in front of my eyes. Philip, dead on the floor. Children running. Children running everywhere. The girl sitting on the floor. The expression on Joanne's face at the first shot. So surprised, so bewildered. My boyfriend, bleeding to death just ten metres away from me. He's watching us now, and I can sense his fear. I'm ashamed, because it is fear for my life, not his own.

I feel empty. In this second, fear disappears. Makes way for something even worse. Indifference. I'm going to die. And it doesn't matter. It's all the same, whether I live or die. Whether I am in pain or not. It's over now. I wait for the shot. I just hope he doesn't find Joanne. At least one of us has to survive.

All this passes through my mind in a single second. A single but very important second. Because, even though it's only one of millions of seconds I have lived through, it seems to me that it lasts as long as my whole life so far.

I hear the shot. And then a second. And a third. Something brushes my right leg. I expect to fall to the floor. But it is Mathias who collapses, two bullets in his body. I think he's dead. He *is* dead. As dead as Philip.

Shaking, Joanne comes out of her hiding place. We stand together as a commando rescue squad comes pouring through the door. Ambulance men and armed police. They're wearing black clothing, kneepads, heavy helmets that look a bit like motorbike helmets. But that's not what is so petrifying. It's the guns. Everywhere. I'm stupefied.

They bend over Toby. Put him on a stretcher and take him away. Everyone's trying to talk to me and Joanne. They're pointing at my wounded leg, my bleeding arm, but I just shake my head.

And then I run after the stretcher, ignoring the protests of my leg. He's still alive. I saw. His chest is still rising and falling.

I run past a lot of people, through the school building. Until I reach the door, where I see the ambulance men disappearing with Toby. I want to follow, but then I stumble back.

It's terrible. I wasn't expecting anything like this. Journalists. So many journalists. With their microphones and cameras. They're filming us. Filming us as if it's one of those goddamn blockbusters you see on TV.

Stunned, I just stand there. Then I run to the ambulance that they are pushing Toby into. I'm almost there when I am stopped by a reporter. 'Hey, little girl. Tell me what happened in there. ... Hey, wait a minute!'

I ignore him. What he wants doesn't matter. There's something more important.

'It'll only take ...'

'Hey, what are you doing here? Please stay behind the barrier. And leave the children alone!' A policeman is standing next to me, shooing the reporter away. I search the carpark with my eyes. But the ambulance has gone.

Toby's gone.

I want to cry. There's this pressure. Everywhere. And I know that tears could help to release it. But I can't. I just let myself fall. Sit on the asphalt and stare straight ahead.

More and more people are coming out of the school. Children, girls like me, Toby's pals, teachers. We all look the same. Like ghosts.

Joanne sits down beside me. We say nothing. What do we have to say? Nobody takes any notice of us. Nobody comes to treat my leg. Because there aren't enough medics. And way too many wounded. I've counted three dead bodies so far. And some children look way worse than me.

I lean my head on Joanne's shoulder and we sit there like that. Waiting for … something. For nothing, for everything, for a miracle. To wake up? Do we think it was all a dream? It wasn't. *Isn't.*

CHAPTER 3

Somebody bandages my leg, takes care of my arm. My dad is here. He wants to help me. Toby's mum comes. Toby is dead. Died on the operating table.

I hear all this as if through a fog. I ought to be crying. Reacting. But I can't. It all seems so unreal, so wrong.

Is it really real? I can't understand how it could be. It's just a normal day, like any other. Everything is the way it always is, or at least it should be like that. What on earth has happened?

Joanne leaves. Her parents take her away from here. Dad puts his arms around me. Grandma and Grandpa come, and they hug me too. But even that feels false, wrong. A lot of cameras and journalists have turned up. They put their microphones under our noses, film the school.

I just switch off. I can't see anything, hear anything, feel anything. *Nothing at all.* Not even the beating of my heart. No horror, no fear. Nothing. I don't even feel the pain in my leg any more. Not even Grandma's hand, resting on my shoulder. They could just leave me here for the rest of my life, it wouldn't matter to me. Nothing matters.

My grandparents and my dad take me away from the school. The journalists are getting in our way. I don't react. But Grandpa shouts at one of them at one point. I don't know what he shouts.

Suddenly I'm so tired. It's a new kind of tiredness. It's dark and heavy and very, very sad.

I don't want any more. I don't know what it is that I don't want. That sentence just arrives in my head and won't go away.

I walk mechanically, holding my grandma's hand, following Dad and Grandpa. I have no idea how long it takes us to get to the car. Maybe half a minute or maybe a whole hour.

To think of nothing. I've never been able to do that before. I couldn't even imagine how. Now I'm doing it automatically. I'm empty.

Grandma sits beside me and fastens my seatbelt. I'm behaving like a baby. I don't react. Grandma has to unfasten my seatbelt too and lead me into the house. I've never felt so apathetic before.

This morning, I ran out of the house, feeling chirpy, thinking how nice our house looks in the light of dawn. Now it looks like any house. A lump of concrete with rooms that can lock you in, so that terrible things can happen in them.

Grandma leads me into the bathroom, undresses me,

puts me under the shower. The warm water flows down my body. My cold, numbed body.

I try to understand what I've seen. I really try, but it doesn't work. There is nothing I can compare it to, what I have just experienced. It's all so unreal.

I shiver when Grandma gets me out of the shower, even though the bathroom is steaming. The cold comes from within.

Grandma puts jogging pants on me and a sweatshirt and gets my snuggly red socks, which she knitted for me. But I'm still cold. It comes from within. From deep inside, where nobody can reach.

Grandma puts me to bed and tucks me in. And because I'm still shivering, she gets two extra blankets for me. Then Grandpa comes and slides a hot-water bottle under my cold feet.

The two of them leave, and then Dad turns up. He strokes my cheek. But he says nothing. He just sits on my sofa in the corner and waits. And waits.

What's he waiting for? A miracle? For me to get up and say, *It was all a joke, Dad*? I wish it were. That everything felt normal again. This morning seems like ten years ago. Or like a totally different life.

Can it really be only five hours since I thought the worst thing about the day was that I had to *get up* at six o'clock?

It's all so unreal. As if it's a film. And the awful thing is, I'd have liked watching this film.

And now I'm living through the nightmare of the main character. Just like the other 1024 other pupils in my school. That can't be right. There are fewer of us now. Who knows how many are still alive?

I can't really describe it to you. You'd think, wouldn't you, that you'd have lots of things to think about and to feel when you've had an experience like this, such a disruption to your life. But it's not a bit like that. It's probably the shock. My head feels as if it has been swept out. And I am so endlessly tired.

You're probably amazed that I can sleep. But, oddly enough, I can. As soon as I close my eyes, I fall into a deep and dreamless sleep.

I'm grateful that I was able to sleep. Because as soon as I wake up, I'm right in the middle of life.

I was woken by a sound. Something fell. It echoes in the dark. Then I open my eyes. I can see my bedroom ceiling.

I know that if I look around my room, everything will be the same as it always is. My furniture will still be there. The walls are still blackberry-coloured. My posters of P!nk and Green Day and the photos of my girlfriends will still be hanging there. Me and my dad on his fortieth birthday are framed in a silver photo frame on my night-stand.

Everything is the same as it has always been. And that

is precisely the problem. I feel the whole world should be different now. The sky should not be blue but green. And leaves should be black. Our house brown instead of white. My hair not straight but curly.

Everything feels different. So why hasn't everything changed too? How come our house is still standing? Why are Joanne, Vanessa, Sophia, Tanja and I still grinning in the pictures on the wall? We should be crying.

I sit up. Run my fingers through my tangled hair. My lip is gashed and it tastes salty. My pink nail varnish is flaking. Everything feels so intense. My head is clear, from the very first second. I know immediately what has happened.

Toby is dead. Gone for ever. As if he were never there. A person can't just not be there any more. A person doesn't just disappear like that. Our last minute together was so dreadful, it can't really have happened.

I have often felt lonely. Because my mother ran away, because Dad has to work so much, because Grandpa has to be in hospital so often. But all that is nothing compared with the loneliness I am experiencing now.

I've just noticed that Grandpa is sitting there on the couch. He looks at me with old, knowing eyes. And I almost believe he knows how I'm feeling. But nobody can know that. Except maybe those who were there with me.

He clearly doesn't know what to say. What does anyone say after such an event? It's a bit like that time when Grandpa found out that he had a tumour in his lungs. It's the kind of moment where you can't say a single thing. Then, I remember it still, I just whispered, *I'm so sorry*.

But I don't want Grandpa to say that to me now. It would sound as if I were sick. As if there'd been an accident or something. I couldn't bear those words.

'Just don't say you're sorry,' I say very softly. Grandpa stands up, takes the water glass from my table and offers it to me.

'That's fine. I won't say anything.'

Thirstily, I put the glass to my lips and empty it in a single gulp. I realise that my lips are burning. I lick the huge dry spots. That's a good feeling.

The pain, such as it is, feels real. And ordinary.

Then I see in front of my eyes the first moment after the rampage, the first that I can grasp. For the first time, I don't feel like an onlooker.

To *go on the rampage*. That's not a phrase you use every day. Sure, the boys in my class used to joke about it. Also, we've definitely seen a film about someone running amok on a gun rampage. But what you don't see in these films is how you are supposed to feel after someone has gone on the rampage. How you're supposed to behave. How you're supposed to interact with your family. And how the family is supposed to deal with it. The situation I'm in is a bit like as if I landed up in a strange country without a map and not knowing the language. I haven't got a plan.

Something terrible has happened. And now what? What happens next? How are you supposed to go on?

The best thing would be for me to just stop thinking. But my brain simply keeps on working, unbidden, without stopping. I believe I'm doing something wrong. I don't feel a thing.

Grandpa looks desperate. It's probably not easy for my grandparents or my dad either. But I need a moment to myself.

'Grandpa, will you make me a hot chocolate?'

He just smiles and goes. As he leaves the room, something fizzles out inside me. An incredible pain starts and I curl up. I'm breathing loudly and fast. But not a tear flows down my cheek. Slowly, I try to calm myself down.

I think about the exercises that Grandma taught me. Because I never slept well as a small child. I think about forests and happy hares and fields. About the wind blowing through my hair, and the sun shining on my face.

Bad thoughts keep creeping in, though. And what now? *Miriam*, they whisper. *What are you going to do now that your boyfriend is dead, and all because you did nothing?*

I don't want to hear that. I don't want to think that. It doesn't go away, though. The pressure in my heart just won't dissolve. It's so hard to breathe. Every rise and fall of my chest hurts.

I sit like this for a while, concentrating only on not listening to the accusations I make to myself. Then I get up and go into the bathroom. The face that looks back at me shocks me. Is that really me? I look like a stranger.

Like a girl I've only just met for the first time.

Eye colour, hair, shape of face. All the superficial things have not changed. But what about the rest? Where does that expression in my eyes come from, this indifferent, defeated look? My face looks so fierce, so horrifying, that I actually feel afraid of myself.

I'm not sick. Yet I'm shivering all over, though I'm not cold. And I'm as pale as only dead people usually are.

I turn on the tap, splash water in my face in order to get rid of the remains of my make-up. I hope that might make me look a bit healthier. I turn to my wall mirror and pick up my hairbrush. Carefully, as if I can't trust myself, I pull the brush through my tangled hair.

My body is weak. My legs look like matches. I wouldn't be surprised if I just collapsed on the spot. I hold on to the wash basin. Keep breathing. No matter what, just keep breathing. If anyone had told me it could be so difficult I wouldn't have believed them, might even have laughed at them. Breathing. Our bodies do that automatically. All the same, it can be very wearing.

Don't ask me how long I stand there staring at myself. I've lost track of time. What time is it? How long did I sleep? How long have I been standing here?

I decide to go downstairs, to my family, so that Grandpa doesn't have to bring the hot chocolate upstairs. I just want to be hugged by them, not to be alone any more.

The stairs creak as usual in a particular place. Softly, I move towards the kitchen. I have no idea what is ahead of me. How are they going to behave? I've never felt so unsure of myself in my whole life.

Voices are to be heard. My heart is beating in my throat. All I want is for them to help me and make me feel better. I press down on the door handle and enter the kitchen.

Naturally, I expected my grandma to hug me immediately. But the person who calls my name and falls on my neck when I open the door is not my grandma. And not my dad either.

My mother is there in front of me, after staying away from us for so many years, and she's hugging me. Under normal circumstances, I'd have pulled away from her. She shouldn't touch me. But I'm too weak.

For so many years, I hoped she might come back and I'd have a mother again. And later, after I'd learned how to get along without a mother and my hate for her had got greater and greater, then I wanted to see her once more so that I could tell her all the horrible things I feel.

Now she's here, and I don't care.

I stiffen and wait for her to let go of me.

'How long did I sleep?' I ask my dad, tired.

It must have been a long time, if my mother had time to get on a plane from wherever and get here.

'Almost a whole day. Your mother came because she's been worried about you. She took the first flight, as soon as she heard.'

My mum has come because she's worried. I can feel the

anger rising in me. So now she's worried, but for the past five years, she didn't worry at all. She should go back to wherever she's come from.

I wanted to find refuge with my family. Instead of that, I have to look my mother in the eye. Surely they know that Mum is the last person I need?

I just want some peace.

There's a thousand things I could shout at them. But I'm too meek, too feeble. So I just ask, 'Why?'

Actually, it doesn't really matter. It's all the same. If she wants to stay here, well, anyone can come and go as they like. I just want to go to my room, to my bed, and do nothing. Nothing at all.

I glance at my mother out of the corner of my eye. She looks just the same as before. Five years, and she hasn't got as much as a new wrinkle. Only her skin has got darker from so much sun. And she's had her hair curled. Her neckline is way too low-cut. And her God-knows-how-many piercings. Her red-lacquered fingernails. She's really back.

Toby should be here. He should put his arms around me. Then I'd feel a lot better. I *need* him. Words can't express how much I need him. Such a wonderful person can't just die. It can't just be that I will never see him again, that there is just no more Toby in the world. What is a world without Toby? I am gripped by a deep despair. The kitchen, my family, my recently returned mother all fade into the background.

'Darling, I know we haven't the best relationship, but I thought …'

I take no notice whatsoever of what my mother is saying. Her words and her opinion are of no interest to me.

'Miriam, your mother is here to help you. We all want to help you.'

Where did they get the ridiculous idea that my mother could help me? What makes them think any of them could help me? Nobody can do that. Not them, not myself. No-one. Do they not get that? Is it so hard to understand?

What has happened is savage. People have died. Toby is dead. And they are talking about wanting to help me. I can't really explain what's happening inside me at this moment. It's just that I feel pretty empty, and my whole body hurts.

A few minutes ago, I hoped that my family could help me. But that's stupid. Nobody, *nobody* can help. There's me and there's the day just past, which brought terror. And in between, there's nothing.

I run to my room. Mum and Dad follow me. I take absolutely no notice of them. They can say as much as they like. It is unimportant. Like everything else. Like me. In the end, everything in life is unimportant, and what's not unimportant has been violently torn away.

I bang my door and lock it. Then I collapse and curl up in a ball. I rock myself back and forth to calm myself.

Rampaging. No, it can't have been that. That sounds so unreal. Rampaging sounds like America. You keep hearing about people going on the rampage in America. Someone can't have gone on a rampage in my school. That kind of thing doesn't really happen. And why should I, of all people, experience such a thing? What really did happen yesterday?

CHAPTER 4

Life is like a very long breath. You breathed out at some stage and have no more air in your lungs. Then everything is empty, everything is over. But I wonder, do we humans die only one death? Or do we live through many little deaths?

They say cats have nine lives. Maybe we humans have the same. Maybe there is a certain amount of pain that we have to live through until we are put out of our misery.

I always thought it must be hard to die. But Philip has shown me that it's easy. The easiest thing in the world. Like breathing out. It happens by itself.

People are scared all their lives of the moment when it all ends, and then it turns out to be so easy. I'd rather worry about tomorrow. Or the day after tomorrow. Because it's life we should be afraid of. Death is a release; it's life that brings us to our knees.

Living is hard. Because you die doing it. And then you are a totally new person. A person you don't know at all. A person you can't abide.

I just lock myself in my room. I'm guessing I've been

here about three days. I don't know. I can't tell by the light, because I've left my shutters closed. Only my reading lamp throws a small, bright patch on my wall.

I don't sleep. Because I only dream of terrible things. Even the relief of sleep has been taken from me. I don't eat. They do keep putting things outside my door, but I don't touch it. I just sit on the floor and don't do anything at all.

The old Miriam would definitely have found that boring. But I'm not the same Miriam. I've changed. And now when I look at myself in the mirror, I know that I'm going to have to change outwardly also. Because I can't stand it any longer.

I can't stand my family either. They keep knocking at my door. They want me to open up and talk to them. But what would I talk to them about? They just couldn't understand how I feel. They keep saying I should meet them halfway. That I should help them so that we can all get through this together. But they are forgetting something very important. This is my thing. Not theirs. It doesn't matter whether or not I tell them. I have to face this myself. And for the moment the best thing is not to talk to anyone, not to see anyone.

Lord, there they are knocking again.

'Miriam, sweetheart, just open the door. And at least eat something. If you don't want to do it for your own sake, then at least for us.'

For us. They keep saying that. I should do everything

for them. But this isn't about them. It's about me. And they just can't accept that.

I just take in the bottles of water that they leave outside my door. That's the only indication that I'm still alive.

They talk to me, but I don't hear them. I've learnt how to do that recently. To turn off my hearing when I want to. I do really still hear. It's just that my brain doesn't register it.

'Miriam, let us at least check your wound. We need to know that everything is all right. Come on, it must be hurting.'

Is it hurting? I don't know. It's nothing compared with the hole in my heart. I keep hearing that shot. Then I feel so sick I think I'm going to vomit. I keep seeing Toby lying on the floor, so pale, and his blood is everywhere. I keep seeing Mathias Staudt in front of me, the gun turned on me. If the rescue squad had arrived even a few seconds later, I'd probably be dead. And I'm not sure how I feel about that. There's this sharp pain because I have this thought that just won't go away. Maybe it wouldn't have been so bad at all to die. Then I'd be with Toby. Then I wouldn't have to put up with Mum. Then everything would be better.

Time is surreal. Did you know that? I didn't – till now. On the one hand, a minute feels like an eternity, and on the other hand a day feels like the blink of an eye. And all this time I have these thoughts. They are wrong. I should be glad to be alive. I'm sure Toby would like to be alive. But a life without Toby? What is that? If I could, I'd swap with him. I don't want to live like this. I don't want to feel all this.

How long ago can it be now since the shooting? It feels like a lifetime. Really. As if I'd died and now I'm living a new life.

Nothing is like it was before. Not drinking. Not sleeping. Not feeling. Not even breathing. A moment that changes everything. Life before doesn't count any more. It is just gone. As if it never existed.

These pictures are hanging in my room, in which girls are looking, laughing, into the camera, and I wonder who these girls are. I can see a girl who looks like me. But I don't know who she is. Where has she gone? She can't just have disappeared. She must be there, somewhere inside.

I search and search and search. In vain.

Who am I? Who am I today? I used to be a happy and beloved schoolgirl with average grades, a super-sweet boyfriend and the best friends you could wish for. But I can't find this girl any more. I've lost myself. I'm in the same body as before, I have the same name, I'm still me, but at the same time I'm not. Because somehow I'm totally different from before. Changed. Not myself any more.

Toby could tell me who I am. I could fill a whole page with reasons why I need him, why he should be here. But it wouldn't be any use.

We all have someone or something that is more important than anything else on earth. For some people, that might be money; for others their child, or their work. For me, it's Toby.

I could follow these thoughts for ever. But I can't go one step further. I have no idea why I can't take another step. The room seems to be oppressing me. The walls are coming in on top of me. I can't stand it any longer.

So I leave my room. On the landing it's just as dark as in my shuttered room, but there's a light down in the living room. My mum is talking to my dad. I can hardly believe she's still here. It's almost a miracle that she's stayed in the same place for so long.

I go quietly into the kitchen, so that they can't hear me. I can do without the pair of them. Mum is ... well, she left me before. And my dad is no better right now. After all, he's the one who brought her back. Him of all people. Has he forgotten how badly she hurt him? I don't understand him.

Even though I'm not hungry, I get a yoghurt out of the fridge and sit on the kitchen counter and start spooning. I haven't turned on the light, I'm sitting in semi-darkness.

The yoghurt makes me feel sick. I haven't eaten anything for days, and I still can't get anything down. I start to gag. My body's survival reflexes seem to have disappeared as totally as the rest of me. Or else my body has decided to starve me to death.

I could just stop, of course. It wouldn't be so bad. If it

stays the way it is now, I wouldn't even feel hungry and so everything would just come to an end.

When the light goes on, I have to shut my eyes. Because I'm totally blinded for a moment. After a few moments I dare to open my eyes again. My mum is in the kitchen. Wordlessly, she sits down at the little kitchen table and lights a cigarette. She says nothing, I say nothing.

Sometimes you don't need any words to have a conversation. Sometimes silence says more than a thousand words. The old Miriam liked to talk a lot. The new Miriam prefers to keep quiet.

If Mum wants to sit here and smoke a fag, that's fine by me. As far as I'm concerned, she can stay here. As long as she doesn't start licking up to me, just because she's suddenly realised she has a daughter. I have enough to cope with myself. I don't want to see anyone. Nobody except *him*. But he can't come. That's impossible. So I'm alone. I'm not interested in anyone else. I only want him. They will say that we all have to work together to get through this.

Why *we*? Was Toby *their* boyfriend? Did they see him dying? And what about Philip? Did *they* hear the shot that killed him? *We* have to get through this, they say, but actually I'm the one who has to get through it.

But the problem is, the only way I could get through this is with Toby. Without him, it's impossible. Without him, there is no reason to get through it.

I let the yoghurt pot fall onto the table. The spoon

clangs on the tabletop. I should not think like this. I don't want to think like this. But I still do it.

My mum stands up and goes to the door. Before she leaves the room, she turns around and says, 'You have every right to grieve. But if you don't eat properly and you don't take a shower, that doesn't make anything any better. At least go to bed. Please. You look as if you are going to fall over with exhaustion.'

I don't care what she says. Does she think I'm interested in how I look? A few nice words don't make anything better either. What does she know about what I need? I don't need anything.

But then I remember what it felt like when Grandma put me under the shower a few days ago. The water felt good. Real, like before. The feeling of water on your skin, that's the same as *before*. It has a soothing effect.

I go into the bathroom. Once again, this strange girl looks at me out of the mirror. I get undressed slowly. I turn the water to lukewarm and let it run over my back. It's nice to feel something again, something good. I concentrate on that.

After my shower, I put on my long blue bathrobe. I comb my hair and brush my teeth. Then I go back into my room and lock the door. I don't want anyone to be able to get into my room in the night. I put my pyjamas on. Maybe sleep would help after all. Not to think for a while, not to feel, that'd be lovely. I snuggle down in my bed and pull the duvet up to my chin.

I really expected that I'd fall asleep immediately, like the last time. But I toss and turn. I keep leaping up because I hear shots behind me.

When I close my eyes, I see the same images. Blood everywhere, bodies lying around me, Mathias Staudt in front of me. I wonder if he'd have felt good if he knew how much he terrorised us. For sure. If there's life after death, he's probably sitting somewhere, laughing because I can't get to sleep.

Damn you, Mathias, I can't understand how anyone could do something like that. OK, so he wanted to get revenge on us. But he dragged others in who had nothing to do with it. And if that doesn't matter to him, he should at least realise that he is hurting his family by doing that. They are going to have to live with the guilt. And himself. Though of course he's dead now too. School would have come to an end, eventually, and he could have got on with life, left it all behind.

I don't understand it. I just don't understand it. All the children. How could anyone do that to an eleven-year-old?

Although my thoughts torture me, I somehow drift into the dreamworld. However, I'd prefer if it were different. Because I dream about my father running through the house, shooting my grandmother.

The first time, my racing heart wakes me. I need a moment before I orient myself. A look at the clock tells me it's only eleven o'clock at night.

Reluctantly, I slip back into sleep and I have another nightmare. This time I'm at school and I'm doing a Latin exercise. Then Mathias Staudt comes in and shouts at me. He says it's all my fault and he's going to put an end to it. Then he stabs me with a knife and keeps doing it.

I wake with a scream. It's only two and a half hours since I last woke.

It takes ages for me to go asleep again. Then I dream about Toby. He says he loves me. But then he starts to bleed and bleed. I want to help him. But it doesn't matter how hard I press my hands to his wounds, I can't save him.

At half past five, I wake again, bathed in sweat, bawling crying. This time I don't try to go back to sleep again. Instead, I go for another shower. That used to help if I'd had a bad dream. Not today.

When I try to dress, it's hard to get it right. There are painful memories bound up in every piece of clothing. So in the end I reach for a black shirt I've never worn before, because I found it too colourless. Under it I put on a printed black T-shirt that I've also never worn because my mum sent it to me. By chance, one more item of clothing falls out. A green cardigan. I hold my breath for a moment. I try to fight the memory, but without success. It pulls me in.

'What should I wear, Joanne? It's a very important date. I want to look perfect.'

My dad is not home this evening and I'm planning to sleep with Toby for the first time. I'm so excited.

'Just put on something you feel good in.'

'But Toby knows all my clothes. I want to look wonderful this evening. I'd like to wear a dress, only it's got too cold for that.'

'Oh, yes, your grey one. It really shows off your figure. You look incredible in that.'

'Yes, but the problem is that it's a halter-neck and –'

I suddenly realise that Joanne isn't running around me any more. I turn around and there she is, a few metres away, staring into a shop window.

'What are you looking at?'

I go over to her and see a short, very short green cardigan, a super forest green.

'Are you thinking what I'm thinking?'

'Otherwise I wouldn't be standing here, would I?' Joanne grins meaningfully at me.

I throw the cardigan back in the cupboard and close it.

Then, with a sigh, I lean against it. I slump with pain. It was so lovely, so uncomplicated. That was my life.

I stay sitting there for a few moments, My whole room is full of memories. Every picture, every object has a story to tell. Some are lovely. Others hurt just to think about them. They hurt because they have to do with Toby. Or with school.

I can't make it alone. I need Toby. But he is not there any more. How can a person just not be there any more? It's impossible. He must be somewhere.

My fingers numb, I reach for the telephone on my little bedside table. Joanne's number is on speed dial, on number 1, even before Toby's.

Nothing happens for ages. It just rings. The tone echoes sharply in my head, emphasising how alone I am with my horrible thoughts.

Then Joanne's mother picks up. Her voice sounds low and fragile. Completely different from the woman I've known for years.

I find it wretchedly hard to speak. The words stick in my throat. Everything feels so strange. I am in contact with the same people as before, apart from my mum. But they seem so changed. Are they really? Or is it just me? Am I reacting differently to people? This thought frightens me.

I close my eyes for a moment and pull myself together. I just want to speak to Joanne. My best friend.

'Hello, Dana. It's Miriam. Is Joanne there?'

Is that my voice? It sounds so hollow. But it has to be mine, odd as it seems.

'Sorry, Miriam. This is not a good time.'

'Oh,' I hear myself say. Then there's an embarrassing silence. 'Could I try again later?'

I can hear a sigh at the other end of the line.

'Maybe another time. She just needs time to herself at the moment.'

'OK,' I murmur, before hanging up.

I can understand that Joanne is not in the mood for playing my amateur psychologist. But she needs a friend to talk too herself. That's exactly what I was hoping for. That we could talk about it. Or about something else. Doesn't matter what. I'd just like to hear her voice. I don't want to be alone. She's the only one who understands me. If I can't tell her about it, I can't tell anyone.

Unspoken words oppress me, stop me breathing. Everything is hurting all at once. A few days ago, everything was fine. Now I can't sleep, eat, think clearly, all because of a single moment. A moment that changed me. But if I have to change, I'd rather do it of my own free will.

Angrily, I make a decision. No, Mathias Staudt is not going to change me. Not completely. Even if everything has changed, I want to be in charge of part of it.

I leave my room, go downstairs. It would be best if I could sneak unseen out of the house without having to explain myself. But Dad is sitting in the kitchen, drinking coffee. Well, it can't be avoided. I'll just behave as if everything is normal. Talk to him for a bit, and then disappear. As long as Dad doesn't want to talk about *that*.

I breathe in. But something holds me back. I can't behave as if everything is OK. I just can't do it. Believe me, I'd like nothing better than to be able to do it. Before, it was so easy to keep things from him. Now and again about a party, sometimes about Toby – and also how upset I was about Mum, so that Dad wouldn't be even sadder.

But this is something else. Something bigger. He won't buy it if I tell him fibs. But I don't want to talk to anyone about it. I can't.

'I'm glad you've come out of your room.'

I shrug my shoulders. Don't say anything.

'We have to talk about what has happened.'

Again, I just shrug. I don't look him in the eye. I knew this was coming. He really expects me to sit down at the table with him and talk about it. As if it were that simple.

'I took the last few days off work. I really ought to go back to the office. But if you like, I could take a few more days off.'

He can't. Dad is a workaholic. He's just saying this so that I will reassure him that my mother and I will work it out between us. I only shrug. He has to decide for himself what's important to him.

'Miriam, will you please say something.'

'Why? What should I say? It's your decision, Dad.'

I hear him sighing and for the first time I look up. He looks desperate.

'You used to tell me what was bothering you.'

'That was then,' I say. Then I leave the kitchen. Why is he forcing me to talk about it? I'll come to him if I want to.

And I will never want to. In the hall, I pull my boots and leather jacket on angrily and fumble in Dad's parka for his wallet and take a hundred euro. He'll be cross. And even more so because not only am I leaving without a word but I'm stealing money from him. Well, then maybe he'll finally realise that you can't have everything you want in life.

It's bloody cold today. It's going to snow any minute. It's the middle of January, after all. The streets look as if they've been swept. After the last few days in my room, the fresh air feels good. Only now do I realise how numb my legs are feeling. My wound is giving me grief too. But the pain is bearable. The cold wind in my face is wonderful. Little white clouds form in front of me.

A bell rings as I open the door. The salon seems scruffy. There's only one other customer there. Three hairdressers are hanging around behind the counter.

'Hello, would you be able to fit me in?' Stupid question. The three of them have nothing to do.

'Hm, come on.' The hairdresser who leads me to a chair seems anything but delighted. 'So what's it going to be? New highlights? Layers?'

She's downright rude. Normally, I'd be irritated by that. But today her gruff manner is just right. As long as she cuts my hair, that's all I want. I want rid of it. If I'm going to be changed, then I want to do it my way.

'No, I want rid of my hair. Totally chopped, so that it's spiky. And red. Really fire-engine red. And a fringe.'

The hairdresser's eyes widen and she fingers my hair. 'Are you sure? Your lovely blond hair? Once you've cut it, it'll never grow this long again.'

Joanne magicked my summer dress, the green cardigan and a pair of black lacy tights into the most fabulous outfit. It was pretty without being too chic. She helped me to curl my hair so that it fell over my shoulders and down my back in ringlets. Only my fringe was plaited back.

Toby couldn't have looked better, in his cool black T-shirt. And his smile, that sweet, crooked smile that he keeps just for me, makes everything even more lovely.

Of course I'm excited. You could see it. I push my hair back nervously. Toby gently touches my parting, kisses me on it.

'Hey, take it easy. You can say stop at any time, you know that?'

I nod. I hide my head in his shoulder. Yes I know that. And it's not as if I never sat on my bed with Toby. We often snogged here. But today it's a bit different.

'I'll never leave you, baby. Really. When I saw you on holidays, it was as if I'd been struck by lightning. And I tried everything to get to know you.'

'You're mad.' I laugh. When Toby talks like this, I always get red. To hide my embarrassment, I kiss him again. I feel very safe and protected when I kiss him. Every time, it's very special, when I touch him, when my hands wander down from his shoulders to his chest and I can feel his heart beating just as fast as my own. My fingers find the hem of his T-shirt and wander under it, feel the taut stomach muscles, expanding at my touch.

Toby pulls his face back a little from mine and examines

me. 'Seriously, Miriam, I don't want you to do anything now that you'll regret later. I love you. I'll wait until you feel ready. We can take our time.'

The more he speaks, the more unsure I feel. His endless chatter makes me nervous and fidgety. I try to calm the two of us down a bit.

'No, we can't.' I smile coquettishly at him. 'I can't take this dress off by myself. And I don't want to sleep in it.'

I take off my cardigan and turn my back to Toby. My heart is racing like mad.

After a moment, I feel cool fingers gently stroking my back and pushing my hair over my shoulders so that they can reach the zip. Then he kisses me so gently that I can hardly feel his lips on my neck.

This little touch makes me warm all over. My neck shivers, and I fight the urge to turn around and kiss him. Instead, I close my eyes in order to experience the feeling more intensely.

'Sure?' I hear the question once again from behind, as his hands stroke my hair.

I laugh and roll my eyes. 'Yes. Sure.'

I think of all the times Toby touched my hair. That time when his lips touched it. When we first met. I think of how he looked then. He made me feel I was the most beautiful and desirable girl in the world.

I think of the first time Toby said 'I love you' to me.

And the way he dispelled all my doubts with those words on that evening when I first slept with him.

If Toby can't see my hair, can't touch it, then nobody else should either. If Mathias Staudt has taken away everything that's important to me, then I don't want the rest of me either.

'Yes, I'm sure. I want it off.'

CHAPTER 5

'Where were you?' I hear my father saying in a panicky voice. At the same time, my grandma shouts, 'Oh, darling, what have you done?'

What have I done? The answer is simple. I've cut my past off. And dyed it. I had to do it and it was the right thing to do. The old Miriam used to glow. Long blond hair suited that stupid little girl. Now I'm older, more mature. Everyone needs to see that.

Of course half the family is throwing accusations at me almost before I've got in the door. It's no more than I expected. They can't understand it. They don't understand me any more. I don't understand myself.

Detached, I put the rest of the money on the sideboard and take off my boots. First accusations, then shouts. The usual family thing when someone is supposed to have done the wrong thing.

Dad asks angrily: 'Where did you get the money?'

Didn't I predict it? As soon as I give him the answer, he's going to get very cross. As if that's going to help.

'Out of your wallet.'

I'm taking my jacket off, so I can't see Dad. But I know he's gone bright red and that that artery of his is bulging.

He should be glad I'm talking to him at all. I'm really not in the mood for this. It makes me laugh to think that a few days ago I was hoping to get help from my family. How very stupid of me!

My father stays surprisingly quiet. 'Miriam, let's talk about this.'

Respect. Not bad. He's learning. After fifteen years he's finally worked out that it is no use shouting at me. With a bit of luck, he'll have worked out that I don't want to talk about things.

'You can call it by its name, Dad.' I hate this fuss. Could we not just go on living? I don't want to be reminded of it all every two minutes. But I don't want to be handled with kid gloves either.

What I'm doing to them now is wrong. I know that. I'm deliberately hurting them, saying cruel things to them, shutting them out. But they don't give me much choice! They're pushing me. Can't they see that? If they'd just leave me in peace, I wouldn't have to be so mean. But they don't get it.

'OK. The shooting.'

I clench my muscles. I hadn't expected this. In spite of my assumed indifference, I can't hide it. I'm not as cold as I think.

I need peace. Too many people, too much excitement. I can't stand it. I'm so exhausted. I don't want to go on blocking them out, don't want to be absent, don't want to wear this cold mask any more. Just peace. To be on my own. In mourning.

My eyes fall on a box in a corner of the hall.

My limbs numb, I go towards it. Even though I have an idea what's in it, I ask, 'What's this?'

'Your things were brought around. What was left at school.'

My school things. My giant pale pink handbag, my exercise books, my brown winter anorak with the fur-fringed hood, my schoolbooks, my mobile, my purse, my iPod, the book I'm reading (a fairly gruesome thriller). Just seeing these things makes me feel sick.

'Burn them. I don't want to have them here.'

'Your school things?' Grandpa sounds surprised. 'We can talk about that later. You don't need to bother about that for now. It's not important.'

Mum and Dad are smiling at me. The two of them are standing beside each other and are smiling at *me*. Together! Whatever they want to say to me, it's not going to be good.

'There's going to be a memorial service tomorrow, and we're to meet in the gym afterwards. We're all going together. You'll be able to meet your schoolmates. You can talk about it. And there'll be psychologists there too. That'll do you good.'

I just stand and stare at them. Oh, it's going to do me good. Now, if my parents are going to say that, they must know what's good for me and what's not. One of them hasn't seen me for five years, and the other one practically lives in his office.

This is really a big thing that they've decided over my head. And there's one thing I'm sure about: I don't want to go to a weird meeting like this tomorrow. I don't want to see my schoolmates. I don't want to see anyone. I'd just like to crawl into a hole.

Easy for them to say what I should do or not do. They weren't there. They haven't a clue. About anything.

I stagger back and bump into the wall. They're watching me expectantly. They want my agreement. As if my refusal would be tolerated. I understand what's going on in their heads. Do they think, *Oh, Miriam has just experienced a killing spree. Now she is mentally unbalanced, so let's plan her whole life for her.*

My father adds insult to injury. 'Miriam, we don't want to force you. We only want what's best for you.'

I snort. Maybe that is really what they want. So they can imagine everything is fine again, normal, if they can just push me into a routine. Even so, they decide everything without me, give me no time to sort myself out. I can't look them in the face, I'm so angry with them. Then my mum pipes up, who so far has only been supporting my dad's point of view with understanding little nods.

'Miriam, it's not up for discussion. You'll go to this service. You won't lock yourself in any more and lock everyone and everything out. And you'll pay your father back.'

I stare at her, open-mouthed. But not just me. Grandpa, Grandma and Dad are just as surprised as I am. I've never known Mum like this. So forceful and so didactic. Like a proper mother.

And this tone of voice. This patient, overfriendly tone of voice. It's my life. It has nothing to do with her. It hasn't even been a week. My family can't expect me to be back to normal. They can just shut up!

'What makes you think you can talk to me like that? Have you even the slightest idea of what I've been through?' Yes, it irritates me the way my family treat me so carefully. But Mum doesn't have to be the complete opposite. *She* can't talk to me like that. 'You can't just start interfering in my life!'

'I'm still your mother!'

Super. Standard comment.

'And where were *you* the whole time?' I yell at her. I didn't know I could shout so loudly.

'Miriam,' murmurs Dad softly. 'Please.'

I take no notice of Dad. Telling the truth obviously isn't allowed.

'You were never here, Mum. You have no right to start behaving like my mother now. Go back to your beach or do something else. I don't care. As long as you get out of my life.'

These words seem to leave my mother completely cold.

'Go to your room. Supper is at six. And tomorrow the service starts at nine. We're leaving at half past eight.'

Had she heard me at all? I'm being treated like a naughty child. But I'm much more mature than my mother. My mother couldn't handle her responsibilities, which is why she bunked off. It's inconceivable that she thinks she can talk to me like this now.

I ought to stomp angrily into my room and bang the door. Instead, I slip past them and close the door softly behind me.

I feel the urge to ring Toby again, tell him everything. Then he'd come around and put his arms around me. And everything would be OK. Not that the stress would be forgotten, but with him, everything would be just much more bearable.

I lie on my bed and stare at the ceiling. Before I was with Toby, being alone didn't bother me. I always thought that I didn't need a boyfriend. Sure, if a super-sweet guy came along, I wouldn't say no, but I wasn't on the lookout. Well, the super-sweet guy did come along.

Now it's terrible to be alone. I'm only realising now how dependent I am on him, now that I haven't got him any more.

I can't help it. I have to do it. I have to hear his voice. With trembling hands, I take my mobile out of my pocket, look at the blank screen.

All I have to do is press on the number 2. As simple as

that. But my finger falters on the buttons. There's a line that I can't cross.

Suppose his number doesn't exist any more? Or if someone else answers? His mother, for example. I can't speak to her.

But the desire to hear him one last time is far greater than any fear.

I listen as a connection is established between the two networks. My heart is beating like mad. It can't have taken more than twenty seconds before Toby's voicemail kicks in, but it feels like an eternity.

Then, finally, I hear him.

'Hi, it's Toby. I can't pick up my mobile just now, but don't bother leaving a message. I never listen to my voicemail.'

At the beep, I hang up. I feel empty and very, very lonely. I roll up into a ball and think about the service at which they'll pray for Toby. I'm afraid of that.

What awaits me tomorrow? What is it going to be like to see all the teachers again? And all my schoolmates. And the walls, where the blood was. And the floor on which the bodies lay? And the classrooms where Mathias Staudt sat?

What will it be like to see Mathias's parents? And Toby's parents. How will Joanne behave? And my other friends?

I don't know if I should be pleased to see them. We've all changed. We're all really too old now to go to school.

How quickly you can age.

I think the worst thing about this week is all the unanswered questions, the uncertainty. I can only stand still and not go forward, because I don't know how.

A schoolmate shot at us. He shot my boyfriend. A boy did that. A boy I passed every day. A boy I went on a school trip with when we were in fifth grade.

I try to understand why a person would do such a thing. But I can't. Probably because there is no reason for it. There's no explanation for violence. He just did it. And now Toby is gone. For ever.

I make myself even smaller than I already am, lying there in the foetal position. Then I pull the bedclothes over my head.

The world feels safer here. More manageable. Warm and secure. Not as if a person you think you know could threaten you with a gun.

When the knock comes at the door, I am quite startled. I have no idea how long I've been lying under the covers.

'May I come in, Miriam?' It's my grandpa. I'm really glad that he's outside my door and not my parents.

'If you must.' I come reluctantly out from under the bed covers and sit up.

He's definitely going to tell me that he understands me. That if he were me, he wouldn't want to go to a service like this either. But that, even so, it's for the best. I can do without these totally helpful phrases.

He comes into my room smiling, closes the door quietly behind him, sits on my bed. It could almost be like before. Because we've had these situations so often. Every time my dad and I had a fight, Grandpa came to talk to me. He understood me, nearly always found a compromise that Dad and I could accept.

This time, he can't understand me. Maybe he can imagine it. But nobody who wasn't there can understand it.

'Nobody can make you go, Miriam.'

He takes my hand in his. I look at it carefully, see for the thousandth time the differences. My pale skin and his, brown with age, mine smooth, his wrinkled. We are not very similar, either in looks or in personality. But he has always supported me.

'Nobody can tell you what you should do. It's just that your parents think it would help you if you could say goodbye. But if you don't want to, I'll talk to them again.'

Of course he would do that. Dear, good-natured Grandpa. He would argue with them for hours on my behalf. As he's been doing for years.

It's lovely to have a person who hasn't changed, in spite of the last few days. My grandpa is the same as ever. He doesn't treat me differently from before.

'On Monday, school is starting up again. It's optional for the first week.'

I should have realised that sooner or later something like this would happen. School obviously has to start again some time.

Even so, I feel ill. It's the thought of having to enter my school, to see the people, to walk past the place where Toby lay. That's all.

'Classes will be held first in containers,' Grandpa says.

'Why?' I ask softly, though I'm really pleased not to have to go into the school.

'The building is being completely renovated.'

I don't want to go to class. Never again. I can't ever sit in a classroom again and behave as if nothing ever happened. I can't get up again every day and go on living my life.

I'm so tired. I just want to lie down on the floor and do nothing. Let everything pass me by until it all comes, some time, to an end.

'Also,' he says, squeezing my hand and pushing my hair soothingly out of my face, 'there's been an invitation to Toby's funeral.' He looks utterly sad, as if he knows how much it hurts me to hear that. Maybe he really does know.

'I can't,' I whisper, not looking at Grandpa. I'm ashamed of my words. I've lost control of my life. I can't do anything any more. For years, I've accused my mother of that, of not being able to do anything any more, and that's why she disappeared. Now I'm like her. And that makes me ashamed.

Grandpa squeezes my hand. 'Yes you can do it. So far, you've always been able to do everything.'

It would be lovely to believe that. Only it sounds so terribly exhausting. I haven't the strength for it.

'I don't want to go.'

'Well, you don't have to.' He gives me a hug. It feels good.

After a while he goes on. 'We have got in touch with a very good psychologist. She'll help you. And we'll try to do that too. You're not alone. You can do it.'

If he's really convinced that I can do it, why is he bringing this psychologist into it? How can a professional in a trouser suit be of any help?

But I don't say that to Grandpa. I know that he is very worried about me. I can see it in the wrinkles on his forehead. When he's worried, they get deeper. He has enough problems with his illness. How my parents are is of no interest to me. They'll never get it. Grandpa is a bit different.

So at first I say nothing. I can always fight with my parents later.

I couldn't sleep last night. At six, I was so glad to have the night behind me that I got up and got dressed. Black denim skirt, black sweatshirt, black tights. My hair is a total contrast. I still have to get used to the colour and the length.

I piled on the make-up. Then I wiped it all off again. To make myself up today feels wrong. I can't hide my anxiety behind make-up anyway.

I'm just sitting here, killing time. Half past eight is an eternity away. Two long hours. You can think a lot in two hours. So I try to read, but I can't concentrate. Anyway, I find the protagonist's problems ridiculous. So I put the book away. I try to distract myself with music. But not even P!nk can do that with her songs. I lay my MP3 player down beside my bed and just stare out of the window.

I bend my left knee and lay my head on it. I watch the birds that land on my windowsill and eat the birdfeed that I always put out in the winter. I can see the bare trees swaying in the wind. They're rocking.

What a lovely movement that is. So calming, hypnotic. No matter what happens, the wind always rocks the trees back and forth. That will always happen, as long as this world lasts.

I fell asleep while I was thinking this, and my grandma wakes me. It did me good to sleep briefly and dreamlessly after the night I'd had. No accusations, no bodies, no shots and wounds. Just falling asleep and waking up with nothing in between.

So Grandma and Grandpa are here again. My conscience pricks me. They have their own life too. Their own house to look after. And Grandpa has to go to hospital all the time. He mustn't forget that because of me.

Tiredly, I rub my eyes. Then I follow Grandma downstairs. Slip on black shoes, pull on my black leather jacket. Everyone's waiting for me. Grandpa is wearing a black suit. Dad too. Mum has a black dress on. Surprisingly, it's totally innocuous. It hasn't got a low neckline, it's not too short. Grandma's trouser-suit is also black.

As we go out and get into the car there's not a cloud in the sky. The sun is just rising. It feels like rain.

Today we're going to think about the victims of an evil deed. Today, everything I've been locking myself away from in the last few days is going to come up again. So why wouldn't it rain? It always rains in scenes like this in the movies.

It's quiet in the car. We're all thinking our own thoughts. I'm swinging my foot nervously. I keep kicking Mum and Grandma who are sitting beside me on the back seat. Neither of them says anything. Maybe they understand. Or maybe they just don't notice.

I wish I were somewhere else as we stop in the church carpark. Before I get out of the car, I swallow one last time. My heart is knocking against my ribs. My hands are damp with sweat. What's going to happen in the church?

We've got this far. Even though I never wanted to have anything more to do with it, I have to get out now to face my schoolmates, my teachers, the ones who know what it's like.

There are probably good reasons why the city has

organised this. Just as there are good reasons why my family insists on my coming. But these reasons are a mystery to me. It's not important. They're not important. I'm not important. We're all unimportant. Because everything is unimportant.

Cold air envelops me as soon as I get out.

Little groups have formed outside the church. The grownups are talking quietly to each other. Their children, my schoolmates, stand around, lost. They don't know any more than I do what they should do with themselves. Birds have landed on the trees and are twittering away merrily. I'd like to scare them away.

'Can we go straight in?' I ask.

The atmosphere inside the church is totally different. Nobody's talking. You can just hear the sobs of the mothers. And the weeping of the fathers. The weeping of brothers and sisters and schoolmates. In here, you'd think the whole world was weeping. For the victims of a rampaging gunman. I'm not quite sure, because I can only see her back, but I think Philip's mother is sitting in the front row.

I stay still for a moment. Then I follow my family into the second last row. There aren't many spaces left. Some people are going to have to stand. I've never seen the church so full, not even at Christmas.

I can see some pupils that I know. Vanessa is there. She gives me a hesitant wave. I wave back, glad to see one of my friends. She's got very thin over the past few days, especially in the face. It's incredible what a few days can do to you.

The last stragglers make their way slowly into the church. Actually it's a pity that something as terrible as death is mourned in a place as gorgeous as a church. But death is part of life. We can't avoid it.

Are you afraid of death? Do you wonder how you're going to die? In the end, it doesn't matter, it's just over. So why live with the fear your whole life? Why think about it all the time?

Do you wonder about that sometimes? Have you got a solution? If you have, could you tell me? Because I keep thinking about death. I keep hoping I'll just go to sleep and not wake any more. So if you have an answer, then tell me about it. Because I haven't got one.

The doors are closed. The preacher goes to the altar and speaks. I can't hear him properly. I'm too deep in my thoughts. Something about 'bad' and 'dramatic' and something about how God looks after us all and how the dead people are with Him now. He also says how many are dead. Seven. Seven children are dead. Then we say the Our Father. When we get to 'Thy will be done,' I have to suppress a snort.

As if something like gun rampages, war or famine could be willed. That would make God very cruel. Proof that there's no such thing as God. Not for me. It's a lie, to sit here pretending. We are pretending that something so terrible has never happened. But in reality, things like this happen all the time, daily, at this moment, somewhere on earth. Violence is the most senseless thing in the world. And even so, it goes on somewhere. For ever and ever. It will never end. Not for us, not on this earth. Violence will never stop. Ever.

It's people who produce violence. It's our own fault. With our egotism and our stupidity, we make life hard for each other.

The president stands up from one of the front rows. There's a low murmur. He walks up to the chancel and starts speaking. Another speech that won't change anything. When it comes down to it, it's all about making a good impression in public. How we're feeling is of no interest to anyone. Nobody asks us if we mind our memorial service being filmed. That's just what people are like. They're really only interested in themselves. Maybe they can't put themselves in another's place. Maybe none of us can.

'Wait a minute!' I shout out over the church square. I don't care that everyone turns to look at me. I don't care about them. I only care about one person, and she is ignoring me.

With quick steps, I walk after Joanne. I almost run. But she doesn't look around. She just follows the gravel path to the carpark.

Looking straight ahead, she wriggles her way between

the lines of parked cars to her parents' car. It is not difficult to catch up with her. She's not trying to run away from me or anything like that.

When I reach her, I touch her on the shoulder. 'Joanne, what's wrong?'

I want to know why she's ignoring me. Right now, I need my best friend ... and it must be the same for her. So why is she setting her face against that?

She looks right through me. For a moment, I really do feel as if I'm in one of those films where people die without realising it. They wander the earth as ghosts, not knowing that people can't see them. It's just like that. Joanne just doesn't recognise me. She is somewhere else.

I feel empty, weak. Maybe I should try again. But I absolutely have to get away from her. I can feel the pressure behind my eyes and I know I'm just about to cry.

Joanne was there for me for years when I cried. I never had to explain anything to her. She could feel why I was sad. And now it's she who is making me cry. Everything is different.

I turn around and put as much distance as possible between myself and Joanne.

CHAPTER 6

Chairs have been put out for us in the city gymnasium. They fill the hall, all lined up in rows. There's a podium at the front, with a microphone.

Everyone is waiting for us, the students of a school in which something really terrible has happened. But as I enter the gym, it doesn't seem that way. Because the people sitting on the chairs are chattering and jabbering. It all seems ordinary. As if it was going to be a gym display given by the children.

I stop for a moment and take in the whole situation. And then I'm pressed forward by the people shoving. At the edge there are still five seats. My parents make a beeline for them and sit down.

I wonder what the principal is going to say. I wouldn't know what to say. I can't even put the whole thing into words for myself. So how could I do it for so many others?

I'd love to just get up and go. Anywhere. Just away from here. I don't want any part of this. I don't want to hear what the principal has to say. I'd like to stay in my own little world, where I can think, only I'd feel so bad.

All I want to do is feel sorry for myself. I'm not interested in these people's feelings.

Our principal stands at the microphone. It whistles. Then her voice echoes around the hall.

'Students, parents, first I want to thank you for coming today. I know it is not easy for many of you. You've all had bad days. Something terrible happened in this school, which leaves us all speechless. All the more important, then, that we don't remain silent, but reach out to each other, and have a conversation. Believe me, we will discuss the event in depth with your children. This is all new to us, but we will try, with the help of specialists, to work through this event as best we can. And together, we will find a way to tackle this task. To this end, psychologists and therapists will offer group discussions, in which the students can participate. There will also be class discussions every week, to talk about the difficulties of getting back to normal. Of course, specialists will also be present at these sessions. You have already got the list of psychologists who are available to you for one-to-one meetings.

'One thing is sure: nothing will ever be the same again, but we, the staff and pupils, will find a way to come to terms with the situation. Please don't hesitate to ask for help. We are here for you, at any time.'

Euuugh! Can I please go and puke? I have to listen to this! There she stands, in front of hundreds of pupils, and addresses the parents, as if we weren't there. That really infuriates me.

We're the ones who were shot at. We experienced it. And yet she's talking to our parents, not to us. We're the ones who are affected by this. She thinks we're all going to get through this *together*, but she can't even speak to us.

'I don't mean to suggest that there are any easy solutions here. But I'm sure we can do it. That's why we have professional help. Bereavement counsellors are available to the students at all times.'

Really? We have bereavement counsellors available to us. They'll analyse the whole thing. I'd rather talk to a stone. It would understand me better than one of these bereavement counsellors. And at least I'd know that it wouldn't write it all up in a file or tell my father about it.

'The coming months will be hard. And this experience will affect our lives. We'll never be able to forget it completely. But we do have the opportunity to reach out a hand to each other and to help each other.'

I can't believe she's talking the whole time about *us*. It's not easy for her either, I know, but she hasn't a clue how *we* are feeling. Otherwise, she'd talk to *us*, not to our parents.

The boy sitting next to me snorts. I look at him for a moment, then I lean over to him and whisper, 'I'm going to get sick.'

I smile at the boy. He smiles back. 'I heard she's supposed to have locked herself in. She just turned the key of her office. She didn't give a damn what happened to us.'

'Really?' I ask. I hadn't thought she'd do that. As the leader of the school, she should have done something, though I have no idea what. But she certainly shouldn't have just saved her own skin. At the end of the day, she is responsible for us. She has no right to be in charge of this school any more. She should have been there. As principal, she should have been there for us. Where was she?

'Together we'll find a way.'

I'm furious. It's not just anger, though. It's hate. I blame her for Toby's death. Whether that is justified or not. I feel all the hate of the last few days. I want to show it to her. I'm tired of talk. I've want to smack her. I've never wanted to hit anyone before.

'Shut up!' I say quietly, just to myself. But even so, some people turn around.

'Keep quiet,' Mum hisses.

As if a word from me could change anything. Or a word from her. Or our principal's speech. Nothing will change anything. Why should I keep my mouth shut? Or listen? What good will that do?

Suddenly this all seems so stupid. I run outside. Dad shouts after me. I don't care. I can't stand all this. This kind of thing should never happen. Nobody needs to hear the school's great ideas about how to cope with a shooting. That's just not right.

So I just run. I run as if the devil is after me. And who knows, maybe he is. Because a kind of madness, such as

I have never experienced before, makes me want to run and run and run.

I don't stop until I reach the main school building. Out of breath, I lean against the wall.

It's not right to talk about us while we're sitting there. To talk to the parents, even though we are the ones who are affected. It's all wrong. Since Monday, everything has been wrong. Mum shouldn't be here. Grandpa shouldn't be looking after me; I should be looking after him. I should be going to school as usual, meeting my girlfriends, spending time with Toby. But Toby is dead. And I have heard nothing from my friends for days.

We used to know everything about each other. They always used to help me. They always understood when I was cross with my mother. They were always able to give me tips when I had problems with Toby. I could always go around to them if my dad was away and I didn't want to be alone. Now it's as if they never existed.

My breath forms white clouds in front of my mouth. It's so cold. My teeth are chattering. Freezing, I fold my arms across my chest. Even so, it's better out here than in the gym.

I wish I had enough imagination to invent my own dreamworld. A world where everything is good. I'm with Toby. Mum never disappeared, my father doesn't go off on trips for weeks on end, Mathias Staudt doesn't even go to our school. What a lovely world that would be!

But I can't really imagine that kind of thing. My sensible

self won't have it. Maybe it's just too easy to hide in a fantasy world, to flee into it when life gets complicated. It wouldn't be good, I think.

'Everything all right?'

Startled, I turn around. It's my mother.

'What are you doing here?'

Of all people, she has to be the one to come running after me, to see what I'm up to. She gives a smile. 'I could ask you the same. It's pretty cold out here.'

'That's not what I mean, and you know it. Why did you come back at all? You were never there for me.'

'Do your earliest years not count at all?'

I think about the happy years in which we were a family. How we went on trips on Sundays. Celebrated Christmas together. Did homework together. But then that was all over within a single day.

I know immediately that something is wrong. Dad is sitting too quietly in the kitchen, alone in our flat. My mother is not there. There's a cup of coffee in front of him. He must be up a while. The coffee is not steaming any more. It's cold already.

He seems to be waiting for me.

I approach him softly, touch his arm. 'Is everything all right?'

A stupid question. Of course something is wrong. Otherwise he wouldn't be sitting here staring into space.

'I have to talk to you. Sit down, please.'

Slowly, I sit down opposite him. 'OK.'

I don't know what I was expecting. I think, deep down, I knew already. There had been signs. All the same, his words shock me.

'Your mother has gone.'

'How do you mean, *gone*?'

He has to say it. What we both know.

'She's left. Couldn't stand it any longer.'

I don't' react.

'But we'll be all right on our own,' he says quickly. 'We can manage by ourselves. Can't we?'

'Yes.' I give a little smile and raise my head so I can look him in they eye. It hits me, like a blow that takes my breath away. My own mother couldn't be bothered with me. I wasn't important enough for her. So she just drops me, like an object that is too heavy for her. And which is broken, like my trust.

CHAPTER 7

Over time, we forget a lot of things about our lives. But some things are so deeply entrenched in us that we can never forget them. These things often reconstruct us, affect us and our behaviour so deeply that we feel we've died and been reborn.

The gun attack is like that. I know I will never forget it. I know it will change me. I know I died that day. I do pretty much nothing any more. I don't even listen to music. I just sit there, staring at the wall. What should I do? Play Wii? Or X-box? Watch TV? Read? Everything is so superficial. This whole world in which we live. The only thing that is real is friendship, love. And that doesn't last either.

My girlfriends gave me an album of photos of our times together. And photos of me and Toby. School events. Outings. I've pulled it out of my wardrobe. I look at the pictures again.

Joanne, Tanja and me at the Christmas market, grinning broadly, blue mugs of steaming mulled wine in our hands. We're all wearing gloves, thick scarves and hats. We made a game of it. We made a pact. To wear white hats, black scarves and brown gloves. All of us. Our cheeks are red with cold. We're standing by a teddy-bear stall, leaning against each other.

Me and Vanessa in her garden, pruning shrubs. It's not a posed photo. Her sister took it while we were working. We didn't even notice. In the photo, we're holding up lots of foliage, just for fun. That's why the photo is so lovely. Our long hair, brown and blond, blowing in the autumn wind; red, orange, yellow leaves flying around us.

Sophia, Tanja, Vanessa and me at a party of someone from eleventh grade. Glittery tops, curled hair, short skirts, pumps, pink lipstick. That was the first time I ever got really drunk.

Joanne and me at a Linkin Park concert. Black hoodies, black mascara. We're shouting as loud as we can. I was hoarse afterwards, I shouted so much. Joanne too, actually.

The five of us together last winter, building an igloo at Tanja's. It took us five hours. We'd planned to drink hot chocolate in the igloo. We were all bloody cold. But it was a fab feeling to sit in the igloo and laugh about it. Tanja and I both got colds out of it, but it was worth it.

The five of us in another photo. It was taken this summer at the lake. We'd brought everything you need for a lazy day at the lake. Rugs, sunglasses, sun cream, air mattresses, a coolbox full of cola. We lay at the edge of the water in our bikinis, chatting. Sophia forgot to put on suncream and got badly burnt.

They also pasted in a class photo of us all. I was sick that day. The other four wrote my name on a sheet of paper and held it up between them. That was so sweet.

That's all in the past now. In her song, 'That's what we live for', Cassandra Steen sings, 'Everything only happens once, even if it doesn't seem that way.' She's right. We live every moment only once. It won't be repeated. But unfortunately, we don't value life.

Why do we live? Life has to make some kind of sense. There has to be some reason why we are here. I can't believe there was just this Big Bang and then everything happened by chance after that. We can't be living just because something happened to happen I-don't-know-how-many millions of years ago.

Surely I wasn't born just to go to school and then later to work? There has to be more to it than that. Something bigger. A plan that we can't all comprehend.

You know, I never really thought that through before. Everything that was there, was just ... there. But now everything is the wrong way round. Why should I get up in the morning? Why should I talk? Or eat?

Upside-down world. Is there something wrong with me? Or is it just that I've got older, more mature? If that is the case, maturity feels horrible. Time is flying by. It goes, and I'll never get it back. I don't use it, though. Because I don't know what to use it for. I don't see any point in going to school any more. Or going to one of those psychologists either.

I have this feeling in my stomach, as if I'm standing at the edge of an abyss. You know exactly what is coming, but you can't do anything about it.

Even the people who mean something to you don't believe in you any more. They've given up hope. And that's the worst. Because it doesn't matter how much pain you have to bear, how many tears you have to shed, how often you fall down – as long as there is someone to reach a hand out to you, you'll get up again. But nobody can struggle alone.

It's really true that you can't do anything alone. I'm standing alone at the edge of the abyss. I'm going to fall. I know it.

Hi, it's Toby. I can't answer my mobile right now, but don't bother to leave a message. I never listen to my voicemail.

I close my eyes and listen to his voice. I imagine he's here with me, talking to me. He'll give a laugh and then take me in his arms.

But when I open my eyes, nothing has changed. Toby is still dead. Nothing and nobody can bring him back.

That's why I don't open them. The silence in my room is unbearable. The only sound is my breathing, which is way too loud.

After his message comes the beep. I can't hang up. It seems so final. If I break the connection, I'm accepting that he will never come back. But I can't do that. How can I live life without Toby?! It's just not on.

It's the little things that remind me he's gone. The way I don't get texts in the morning any more. The way I don't bother to make myself up at the weekend, because he's not going to turn up unannounced. The way he doesn't help me any more when I have a problem with my computer. The way he doesn't laugh at me any more and say I am like his mother when I get annoyed about his behaviour.

Every time I do something that we used to do together, or when I say something that I know he would tease me about, that's when I miss him most.

And of course when I go to bed alone at night and realise that I will do that every night from now on. I will lie in bed on my own. Without him.

'I miss you,' I whisper into the phone. Tears prickle my eyes. I bite my lip, to keep myself from breaking down. Crying isn't going to resurrect Toby.

Slowly, I press the red button, break the connection between Toby's voicemail and my mobile. He was taken from me. I was robbed of him by Mathias Staudt.

Hate is a pretty extreme word. Mostly when we say *hate*, we just mean that we can't stand a person or a situation. But hatred goes much deeper than just not liking something.

I hate Mathias. Really. I wish he'd just shot himself

alone in his room. Or that he'd jumped off a bridge. Then our lives would still be normal.

I used to feel sorry for him. Well, sometimes anyway. When Toby and his friends were really mean to him. Or sometimes when we teased him about something. I'd sit at home later and wonder why I'd said such mean things to him.

Especially that one time.

I am lying on one of the table-tennis tables outside our school. The sun is shining warmly on my face. We have a free period, and Joanne, Tanja and I are enjoying the last of the summer warmth.

It's the end of October. There's frost at night. But in the daytime, you wouldn't be aware of that. It's a very mild autumn. I'm contented, watching the leaves starting to fall from the trees. The colours are lovely. OK, so at the moment, I find everything lovely. Is it because I've just fallen in love?

'Your permanent grin is starting to get a bit creepy.'

Puzzled, I look at Tanja. 'Huh? I'm not smiling at all.' But as soon as I say it, I realise I *am* doing it.

'Oh, man, you've got it bad.' She laughs and throws one of the jelly babies I'd just got from the vending machine into my mouth. She's right. I'm on cloud nine. Every time I see Toby at school, my heart skips a beat. When he comes over to me and kisses me, it feels like a miracle. I just can't believe I'm with him.

'Come to the loo with me, Tanja?' Joanne gets up and pulls Tanja onto her feet. 'Give her a chance to get over her giggling fit.'

'You better believe it,' Tanja replies, just as I say, 'Hey!'

The two of them disappear. I shake my head, amused. I'm not that bad. Maybe a bit more optimistic than usual, but still, pretty normal. I think so anyway.

I doze a bit and wait for the pair of them. I don't mind them teasing me. I'm so happy, I couldn't care less about anything.

Someone is standing between me and the sun, so that a shadow falls on me. I turn and am just about to say something to my friends. But it is Mathias Staudt who is standing there.

I raise an eyebrow and look him up and down. I don't understand why he always comes to school looking such a mess. I'm not talking about fashion, but about hygiene. How can anyone go around with such greasy hair?

'Yes?' I ask, and I know how bitchy I sound.

'I ... just .. I ...' he stammers.

I give an exaggerated sigh and roll my eyes. 'You're standing in my sun.'

He's a little sheepish. He seems a bit lost, somehow. Well, it's his own fault that people talk to him like that. He's never complained about it.

'It's the dancing class end-of-term ball in a few weeks.

I thought ...' He hesitates again. He's lost his nerve. And he's looking at the floor the whole time. He should be a bit more self-confident. 'Well ... maybe we could go together?'

'What!' It had never occurred to me that he might ask that. I'd heard that Mathias fancied me, but I hadn't really believed it.

I can't help it. I start to laugh. Loudly and meanly. Mathias Staudt wants me to go to the end-of-term ball with him! The end-of-term ball. To which Toby and I aren't even going, because we both hate dancing. That's the first night that Toby is going to spend with me, as my dad will be away on business. And now Mathias is asking me out!

'Now, listen to me,' I say with a snort. I'm trying, in vain, to suppress a laugh. 'Even if I were not entirely happy with my boyfriend and we hadn't already got plans for that evening, I'd rather go to the ball myself than with you. You stink. You have really bad acne and you don't wash your hair. I wouldn't go out with you if you were the last boy on earth.'

I don't know why I give him such a thorough brushing-off. I'm on a roll. I can't stop being nasty to him.

'You look like a pig. And Toby is bloody well like a male model, he's super-sweet and funny and he loves me more than anything. What makes you think I'd want to go out with you?'

Mathias shrinks back. He doesn't say another word. He doesn't look at me. He just leaves. With a hangdog look.

Only then do I realise how badly I have insulted him.

I see him later and I feel terrible. I've treated him like a piece of dirt. I don't much like him, and he should have copped on himself that I wouldn't want to meet him. But I didn't have to be so cruel.

'What's wrong?' Joanne and Tanja are back. They've noticed my guilty face. In stark contrast to my permanent grin.

'Oh, nothing,' I say with a shrug.

I said all those things, and with hindsight I don't even know why. I just did it. It went against my conscience. But I did it anyway.

Now I'm glad. He shot my boyfriend. He shot children. He deserved every word.

CHAPTER 8

Monday. It's exactly a week since the shooting. Only a week. It's been terrible. How terrible is the rest of my life going to be?

The school bell rings. I never thought this day would come. It seemed so far off. But now it's here.

The town square feels empty. Normally, this is where the circus sets up its tent. This is where the city festival takes place. Now, there are rows of two-storey containers on the square. Basically they look like dwelling houses. Only without roofs. There's an outdoor staircase up to the first floor. The containers are at least as big as a classroom. They are not just all the same colour, the way you think containers would be. Green, red, blue, yellow – they look like something out of a kindergarten.

At least half of the pupils are missing. Nobody knows what to do. Nobody has told us how to behave. You read about things like this in the newspaper. See it on television. But you don't see what you are supposed to do afterwards. So we all just stand around. Lost. Confused. Hopeless. Nobody knows if they should approach the others. Some stand around together in groups. Others are walking around the big square on their own. Like me.

I look across the flat, muddy site. So this is where I'm supposed to go to school? It's so different from the mansion of a building in which we used to have classes. Maybe it's not so bad if things are not the way they used to be. Maybe it's good, even …

Hesitantly, I enter the blue container that from now on is going to be my classroom . There are five rows of three tables each, to the left and to the right against the wall, leaving an aisle in the middle. Opposite the door is a board, and overhead projector, even a beamer. It actually looks like a perfectly ordinary classroom. Except for one thing …

It feels lifeless. There are no memories in this room. Notice-boards with reports on them, class projects, class photos. The homework table on the right hasn't been written on. Nobody has drawn anything on it. There aren't any home-made snowflakes on the window panes. The notice-board is bare. There's no photo of the deprived child our class is sponsoring, no dates have been pencilled in. It's a perfectly ordinary classroom, only not *our* classroom.

I shouldn't be sad about it. I knew it would be like this. All the same, it weighs heavily on me. Nothing is like it was before. It never will be again.

I look into the faces of my classmates. I'm not the only one who is unhappy about the new room. With my shoulders hunched, I make my way to the second row, where Joanne and Vanessa are sitting.

Vanessa looks relieved to see me. 'Please tell me you are still speaking to me,' she whispers, softly, so Joanne can't hear.

I smile weakly at her and slump into the place beside her. 'She's not speaking to me either.'

I am as glad to see Vanessa as she is to see me. I turn around and give a quick look around the classroom. 'Where is Tanja? Is she not coming back to school?'

Vanessa looks at the desktop, embarrassed. 'Haven't you heard?' Her voice is muffled. 'They left. Two days after …' She stumbles, but then she makes herself say it. 'After the shooting. She and her brother are with their aunt in Berlin.'

I should feel cross with Tanja. The way she just upped and left! She didn't even say goodbye. But I understand. If I could have done it, I'd have done it too. A new school, where nobody knows what you have experienced. If I'm honest, I envy her.

Our form teacher, Frau Elsenfeld, takes the first period. I can't stand the old bag. She looks like a scarecrow and her personality is no better. She's really cranky. If there's something you don't know in class, she's delighted, and her favourite pastime is writing bad reports. But today, I find her all right, for a change. She doesn't keep talking about the shooting. Finally somebody who isn't making us do something. She just announces a minute's silence. It's actually more like five minutes, and half the class cries through it.

After that, she points at a plain grey box that she's brought.

'This is going to be our worry-box. You can write your thoughts and feelings on a piece of paper and post them inhere. Nobody will read them. It's just a question of writing from the heart. At the end of the school year we can decide what we want to do with it. You can all write your first post now if you like.'

Everyone looks around, embarrassed. Nobody wants to be the first to show weakness. In the end, it's Greta that takes out her notepad.

Gradually, a few others do the same. I get a page from Vanessa (I never have my own note-pad with me), but I'm not planning to post anything in our worry-box. Instead, I write on the paper, before folding it over and push it towards Joanne.

I miss you. Please speak to me.

But Joanne doesn't react. She doesn't even open it. She just stares into space, her thoughts taking her to places where nobody can follow her.

I'd like to shout, right here and now. I'd like to stand

up and yell to the world how I am feeling. So lonely, so powerless.

I can't do it. I can't go to school here every day. Not if Joanne is going to sit right beside me behaving like a doll. Not if the classroom reminds me, day after day, of what I have lost.

Somebody should call *Cut!* and bring the scene to an end, so that I can go back to living my old life.

Class starts properly in the next period. I think that's good. At least everything isn't revolving around our feelings.

At break, Vanessa and I lean back against one of the containers and watch Sophia. She is standing with the dope-heads, smoking. It's a bit cheeky of Sophia to smoke in the schoolyard. How come none of the teachers notices? I don't want to ask whether that's really only a ciggie.

It makes me sad, but also angry. It's one thing not to want to spend time with us, but to dope herself up completely is another. I'd like to clip her on the ear so that she gets it.

'Do you think it makes her feel better?' Vanessa is nodding towards our friend.

I frown. 'Have you seen her? She looks like living death.'

She doesn't answer. She looks so sad, I take her hand and squeeze it. She sighs and gives me a brief smile.

We wait for the bell to ring so we can start back to class at last. I want to have it all behind me, at least for today.

Oh, man! Break always used to be too short. Now it drags out like an eternity. It used to be nice to go to school. There was nearly always something to laugh about. My girlfriends were here, Toby, nice teachers, a fun class, good grades.

That makes me feel sick. As if I am going to throw up. Oh, no! I can't do that now, here, in front of everyone. I force myself to breathe in and out. Everything is fine. As long as I don't think, everything will be all right.

To distract myself, I look at the sky. Is there life after death? Is Toby up there? I hope so. I hope so so much. Then I'd know that Toby is fine.

Toby. Just his name hurts. My heart feels like as if it's been wrung out.

When the bell finally rings, Vanessa comes storming back into our metal box. I want to turn round, but then I see Joanne coming towards me, her face expressionless. I straighten up and stand in her way. She tries to evade me, but I grab hold of her.

'Speak to me. Please. I want to help you.' I give her a desperate look. She takes no notice of me. 'I miss you. Please speak to me.' I can hear the desperation in my voice. The old Miriam would have been ashamed. She'd have been too proud to plead.

My eyes well up yet again. I pinch myself with my free hand. The pain helps to calm me down.

Joanne looks at me then, for the first time since the shooting, and for a fraction of a second, I hold my breath. Her empty stare betrays grief and vulnerability.

Joanne opens her mouth. Her voice is low and cracked. She says only four words: 'Is it our fault?'

I'd like to ask her what she means, but she goes into the classroom without another word.

The bell rings a second time. My legs feel like jelly. I'm shaking all over. I lean against the wall of the container.

Is it our fault?

I mustn't think about it. Joanne is totally off her head. We're not to blame. I didn't press the trigger.

CHAPTER 9

Dr Frei intimidates me. She is a middle-aged woman with very blond shoulder-length curls. She's half a head taller than me. And very thin. Skinny, nearly. She comes across as cool and distant.

But not when she smiles at me. Her smile seems … empathic. Empathic in a way that I can accept, not like my parents.

Dr Frei is someone I might like. If I didn't know that she has a file on me, with everything I tell her in it.

The room is quite nicely furnished. The colours are light, the armchairs comfortable. There are two glasses on the coffee table. There's water in hers, cola in mine. There's even a bowl of sweets, which she offers to me. I'd really like to say no, but I take one anyway. It's a lemon sweet. I close my eyes for a moment and concentrate on the taste. The sour sweet in my mouth reminds me of summer and holidays. Just for a moment, nothing else exists. I open my eyes a tiny bit, ready for what's coming.

'So, Miriam.'

It's starting. Great.

'I hope you don't mind if we speak informally, use first names? It's more relaxing.'

Not particularly. She wants to talk me into trusting her, to lure me out of my reserve. But I am not entirely stupid. It's all the same to me what I call her, because I've promised myself to hate this person, so I just shrug my shoulders.

'I'm Rosalie.'

It doesn't matter. I'm never going to address this woman anyway. I am going to say absolutely nothing during my therapy sessions. I am not going to allow my story to be kept in a file.

'I know you've experienced something very bad. Whatever you're feeling now is all right.'

So she knows I've experienced something bad. Very perceptive of her. Mm, right, that's exactly it.

I watched my boyfriend dying. And another boy. My best friend is behaving as if I don't exist. My mother is suddenly playing super-mum. And to make things even better, she and my dad have decided to send me here. They seem to think I need help. That they can't help me, and that I must confide in someone. Maybe they're right about that. And of course I feel terrible. But that has *nothing* to do with this soul-fixer.

'I can imagine that the whole thing has affected you pretty badly.'

Her understanding voice and her wise look make me sick. What the hell does she know? Was she there? Did she hear the shots? Did she see Toby dying?

An indescribable pain in my chest makes me wince. I've tried not to think about it. I want to get on with my life. Just to forget. Now this Dr Frei is reminding me about it. Whether or not I want to remember.

And it hurts so much. So much that I couldn't cry even if I wanted to. It is a pain that is deep inside me and will never go away.

How could this woman ever understand? I say to her coldly: 'My parents sent me here. That's the only reason I'm sitting here. You don't have to pretend you understand me.'

'So you're not happy that your parents have sent you to me?'

'You're the psychologist. You know the answer.'

I don't know why I'm saying this. Perhaps because I don't want to like her. Or maybe because I'm sorry I've said anything at all to her. I don't want her to know anything about me.

Dr Frei laughs softly. It's a warm and melodious laugh. And that's even worse than if she were laughing at me meanly. I find it hard to hate her when she laughs. She comes across like a friend you could talk to about anything. But of course that's a false impression. That's the impression she *wants* to make. I'm not going to fall for that.

'You don't like talking about yourself. I can understand that. I'd prefer other people not to know much about me either. People can abuse our trust. Sometimes they do that. Nobody's asking you to tell me your whole life story.'

So what am I doing here then? I'd like to ask her that, but I don't. It's better just to say nothing at all. She'll take some kind of psychological view of every reaction, and to be honest, I find that horrifying.

'Is there somebody you can talk to?'

I slump, try to stay in the here and now. I don't want to think about before. But it's too late. The memories pull me in.

I am lying in bed, in my wonderful princess bed. I roll from side to side, laughing. Joanne is lying beside me. She's thirteen. Or rather, she'll be fourteen tomorrow. Tomorrow is her birthday.

I'm jealous. I'd like to be fourteen. But I have two more months to go. Fourteen is better. Fourteen sounds more grown-up, more mature. At fourteen, I'd like to have a boyfriend. Joanne has one. And Sophia has two!

But they haven't ... *you* know. At least, Joanne hasn't. I'm not so sure about Sophia. One day I think one way about her, the next day, the opposite.

Yes, fourteen will be great. And tomorrow, Joanne will have reached it.

'Miriam?'

Our noses are almost touching. And I've drawn the curtains of my princess bed. We often lie here like this and tell each other everything. The others don't know anything about this. Not Tanja or Sophia or Vanessa. It's Joanne's and my secret.

'Yes?'

'I'm really glad I have you. If you didn't listen to me, I'd burst with all my problems. But when I tell them to you, they don't seem so bad.'

I smile. I can't express in words how happy I am to have Joanne. She's my best friend. And I'm sure she's always going to be. We're so alike. Nothing can part us. Nothing and nobody.

That's how I used to think. Before. Two years ago. Before. Last month. Before. In a different life.

'Miriam, is everything all right?'

I don't react. I don't really understand what Dr Frei is saying. I'm thinking about how things were at school today. It was all so strange.

Sophia was hanging around with the dope-heads. She wasn't paying any attention to me and Vanessa has changed too. She used to talk nineteen to the dozen. Today she was sitting quietly in her place. We stood together in break, but both of us were lost in our own thoughts.

Tanja used to cheer us up when we got into a mood like that. But Tanja has left. Will I ever see her again?

And Joanne …? She looks half-dead. Really. She

doesn't speak. Not a single word since that one sentence that I don't want to think about. She doesn't speak, even if a teacher addresses her. She just stares into space, into nothing. I think she's gone mad.

What a week has done to us!

And before I know what's happening, I've gone back into the past again.

'I really hope it's going to snow.'

That's Tanja.

'Yes, all this mud and those bare trees make me sick.'

That's Joanne.

'Are you stupid? It's only November. It can't snow yet.' Vanessa is indignant.

I shake my head, struggling through the woods. Granted, it wasn't exactly smart to wear our Vans in this muck. They're filthy, and our trousers too.

'Mr D, why are we doing this?' Sophia's voice echoes through the whole wood.

Our teacher turns his head towards us. His name is not Mr D, we just call him that, and he's OK with it. He's a cool teacher. Late twenties, with a relaxed style, very easy-going. If he were being measured on some kind of scale of coolness, he'd be a ten. Only thing is he insists on teaching biology.

'So that we can all do something, all of us together, for

the environment. We do it every year. Don't be like that, girls.'

Tanya rolls her eyes and Joanne laughs.

But Sophia isn't letting him away with it. 'Yes, but why are we really doing it? You're not telling me you believe we're improving the world by spending a day picking up litter in the woods?'

I think she's right. This is a ridiculous way to spend a day.

'You're right. We can't make all that much of a difference. But think of it like this. If every ninth grade in Germany clears up once, that does help.'

Sophia shrugs. She's not convinced. But I think about it. He's not far wrong. If every class did a clear-up, then that would help. But the world isn't like that. Not every school co-operates. And even if they did, there are more litterers than there are litter-picker-uppers.

'I think it's all about something completely different,' announces Vanessa. 'It's about finding out how much litter people leave lying around. So we learn not to do it. Isn't that right, Mr D?'

Mr D nods at her.

'Vanessa, who *understands*,' Joanne jokes.

We all laugh. Vanessa is very empathic. That's why we always say that she *understands*. I bet she'll be a psychologist when she grows up.

There are thick grey clouds in the sky and it's foggy. A

really horrible day. And on top of that, now we have to go down this slope. I'm slithering more than walking.

Suddenly, Tanja screeches. Before I can turn around to her, she drags me with her. The two of us roll down a few metres and land in a muddy puddle. We look at each other, smeared with mud. Then we burst out laughing.

Behind us, we hear more laughter. Our whole class is laughing. Well, it does look pretty funny. Mr D is laughing so much he has to lean against a tree.

'You look like pigs,' Joanne snorts. 'Trust you two.'

Tanya and I look at each other for a moment. Then we grab Joanne and pull her down. And then the three of us are covered in muck. But as if that is not bad enough, Joanne takes a handful of mud and throws it at Vanessa. And because Sophia finds that so amusing, Vanessa gets hold of her and pushes her towards us. Sophia drags Vanessa with her. And now there are five of us in the filthy puddle, laughing and laughing and laughing.

'Miriam, did you understand the question?'

Dr Frei's voice seems to come from far away although she is sitting right beside me.

'Sorry. What did you say?'

I feel so weak, so alone. What am I supposed to do about it all? With all these feelings?

In the evening, I log into my Facebook account. I haven't done that since … since Mathias shot at us.

To my surprise, there are more people from my school online than I expected. Some of them are posting about how horrible this day was. Just as if nothing ever happened.

I was hoping that Tanya might be in the chatroom but I can't see her. So I click to write something to her.

For a moment, I stare in astonishment at the screen. Tanya was the last person I wrote to on Sunday. Her details should be there, at the top of the screen. But they are missing.

Puzzled, I type in her name to get to her Facebook page. I can't find her.

Then I realise what's going on. Tanja has deleted herself. She doesn't exist on Facebook any more. I check quickly on Who-Knows-Who. It's the same there. She's gone. She's burnt her bridges.

I stare at the screen for a long time, where her page should come up. Only it isn't going to. Never again. I should just accept that she wants to make a new start. The signs are undeniable. But something in me is not ready to give in. I have to at least try.

I take my mobile out of my pocket and call her. The connection breaks immediately. She's pressed the red button.

I try again and again. And every time, Tanya hangs up at the other end.

It goes on like that for a good dozen times. Then I get a text message:

I'm sorry. I can't.
Please stop trying.

Shit! If she'd accused me of something, that would have been easier. But I can understand. I haven't the heart to ring her again. Instead, I do something that I'd never have thought possible. I delete her number, so I won't be tempted to try again. Now there is no way I can ever contact Tanja again.

Then I finally do what I've been wanting to do all day. I pull the bedclothes over my head.

CHAPTER 10

The next weeks are a blur. The same thing, over and over again. I go to school, and all I do is wait for it to be over. I hardly speak. I go to Dr Frei, and there I am stubbornly silent. But still, she's sure to find something that she can write in her file afterwards. That makes me angry.

At night, I still have bad dreams. It takes me ages to get to sleep. When I finally do, I dream of shooting, shouting and Toby's blood all over the floor. And about my friends. The dreams are so bad that I wake up every couple of hours. I don't know how long I can stand this. I feel alone, numb and empty. And my heart is heavy. As if it has felt too much.

I have to change something. Of course I know that. But I don't know how I can change anything. I think as little as possible about what has happened, but still it keeps nagging at me. I just can't forget it. I'm beginning to wonder if that can ever happen. But if I can't forget it, how can I go on living? How can I laugh, have fun, talk?

Mum annoys me. Suddenly she wants to be responsible, look after me. She is behaving like a normal mother. That makes me angry too. Nothing is normal, nothing. So why is she going on like that? Why doesn't she just go away, leave me in peace?

It's three weeks since the shooting, a Thursday. I feel I can't breathe. School was terrible, but I can't go home either. I feel so weird, no matter where I am.

At first, I wander around aimlessly. Around the pedestrian streets, the park, past terraces of houses, but it doesn't matter where I go, I feel like a stranger. And that makes me so angry. I'm angry with Mathias Staudt, because he shot at us, and with Toby, because he died. With Mum, because she ran away. With Tanja, because she's gone away. And with Joanne, because she won't talk to me. Because she's left me alone with my problems. With Dr Frei, because she's so bloody friendly all the time. But mostly I'm angry with myself. Because I made life hard for Mathias Staudt, and I'm only sorry about it now that I realise what it means to be alone. Because I saw Toby lying bleeding on the floor and I did nothing. I'm regretting all these things now that it's too late. I'll have to live with this. For the rest of my life.

I'm wandering around aimlessly. Only when I stop, I realise where I've been headed. To the graveyard. I wander slowly among the rows of graves. I don't know exactly where he's buried. So I look carefully at the gravestones, looking for his.

We talked about it once. Death. Who'd have thought at the time that it was so close?

The world is spinning around me. The footpath, the traffic, Toby. It all passes me in a matter of seconds, while I spin and spin on my own axis.

I'm laughing. Snow is crunching under my feet. Snowflakes are falling around me; they lie on my hat, my plaits. It's the first snow of winter. The first snow with Toby.

Suddenly a hand grabs me from behind and pushes me against the wall. Toby gives me a serious, half-angry look.

'What is it?' Almost automatically, I touch my hair, my face, looking for the reason why he is staring at me.

Toby shakes his head, annoyed. OK, so he's definitely cross.

'Do you think it's funny to go charging around in rush-hour traffic like a little kid, half a metre from the main road?'

I roll my eyes. Obviously he has no problems in his life. Otherwise, he wouldn't be making such a fuss about me behaving childishly.

'It's not funny! One false step and you'd be on the road and a car would have run you over!'

'Toby,' I say with a smile, reaching for his hand, but he pulls away from me. Man, what is his problem? 'I'm not stupid. 'I can look after myself.'

'Can you really? When you spin around like that, you are about as co-ordinated as you'd be if you were high.'

Why does he have to exaggerate like that? I was enjoying myself. And he's going on as if I had jumped from a 30-metre cliff into a piranha-tank. I'm getting angry with

Toby now; I feel like giving him a piece of my mind. But after all, he is just concerned about me. (Even though it is totally unnecessary.) He means well.

I put out a conciliatory hand to him and after a moment's hesitation, he takes it.

'The probability of my being run over by a car at this moment is decidedly less than the probability that I will kiss you right now.'

I lean forward with a grin. Toby rolls his eyes. Then I close mine and feel his soft mouth. My plan is to smooch a bit, to calm him down. But Toby knows me too well. After a few seconds, he wriggles away from me, holding my two hands tightly, which were just on their way to his neck.

'Do you think I don't know what you're up to?'

I give him an innocent, wide-eyed look, my lips pouting.

He laughs and takes my hand. We walk on. We're on our way to the park. I haven't seen so much snow in December for a long time. The weather forecast says it won't lie long, so Toby and I have to enjoy it while as it lasts.

'I wouldn't be too thrilled if I had to attend your funeral.'

I brush a soft kiss onto his cheek. It is sweet of him to be worried about me. 'Well, I wouldn't be too keen on going to yours either.'

'Since I don't do gymnastics on the edge of the traffic, it's not all that likely.' His thumb is stroking the back of my hand and, although we're almost six months together now, his touch sends a little shiver through me, just like at the very beginning.

'Promise me you won't die?' He's blinking at me, he's not really serious.

I play along. I turn so that I am looking into his eyes. 'I promise, if you will too.'

We're talking nonsense. I could be struck by lightning, slip in the shower, get an electric shock from my hairdryer … There are a thousand ways someone could die, any day.

'I'll try.' Toby is suddenly serious again, stops walking. He takes my face in his hands and kisses me softly and carefully on the mouth.

It's hardly more than a breath of a kiss, but it makes me shiver. I love it when he's like this, when he holds me so gently, as if I were fragile.

I press my forehead to his, and we stand there for a while like that. We look deep into each other's eyes. Something gives inside me. I have no idea exactly what. It just feels suddenly as if I'm light as a feather, as if I could float.

'I don't know what I'd do if you died. OK?' He looks at me with a penetrating look. When we first met, I used to have to look at the floor because I couldn't answer him. It's different now.

I give him an amused and soothing blink. 'Me neither. So the best thing is if we don't die, either of us.'

After a while, I find his name on a black gravestone at the back of the cemetery. I feel tears coming when I see it, but I suppress them. I don't know how I would stop if I let myself start.

To distract myself, I look at the snowy landscape. The hills and the bare trees that spread their branches over the rows of graves. How many people have wept here?

I don't think I really want to know.

You know, you can't describe the sound of gunshot. The moment you lose the boy you love, the moment at which a gun is pointed at you, is the moment that changes everything. In which life seems to be one big lie. What have I done so far with my life? Homework. Hung around with friends. Irritated teachers. Bought clothes. Gone to parties. It all seems so unimportant. All the small-talk we use to drag us through life is unimportant. It's all so *unnecessary*.

People behave as if their lives depended upon it. But now I ask myself what I'm living for. What is the meaning of life? Why do we experience pain and fear, when there's nothing at the end of it? How can there be a future? How can it all go on?

Something in me has changed. A thought is growing in me that I've never had before. I feel like giving up. Just pulling the covers over my head and waiting until life is over. I don't want to be strong any more.

I always wanted to know what it felt like to grow up, to become independent, to get married, to grow old. Now

I don't want to know any more. Because I think that every year just brings new obstacles. I never again want to experience such a devastating blow. For the first time, I think it wouldn't be so bad at all if I died and everything was just over.

This grief that robs me of all other feelings and brings tears to my eyes suddenly disappears. In its place comes a wave of anger. And before I know what I am doing, I scream out, 'You bastard!'

Yes, I'm shouting at the gravestone. Two graves away, an old woman is watching me, horrified. But I don't care.

'Why did you have to die? You promised to watch out for me – always. And now you're dead. Why did you do that to me? Why did you do that to me? Why did you do that to me?'

My voice is trailing away. At the end I'm only murmuring the words to myself. I sink to the ground and rock back and forth.

It hurts. It hurts so much. He's left me. And he'll never come back. Never hold me in his arms again. Never make me laugh. Comfort me. Keep me safe. He'll never smile at me again. I'll never again open my eyes in the morning and look into his face.

And the worst thing is that he's lost to the world. Nobody will ever hear him laughing. Or shouting. Or crying. He's just gone. Disappeared.

'I miss you, Toby.' I turn and go home. I force myself not to look back.

I'm with her again. I hate being with her. This woman makes me nervous. She always looks at me as if she can see right into my soul. Today it's worse than ever. In Dr Frei's consulting room, I feel about as free as a caged animal. I'm running on adrenalin. I feel irritable, agitated. I'm afraid that she knows where I've just been. That is absurd. How could she know? But the thought is still there.

I want to shake my head at myself. I shouted at Toby's grave. What could I have been thinking?

The last few weeks have been terrible. All the same, it's worse today. All the things that have happened recently are crushing me.

Then there's this soft voice in my head, asking why I bother to go on. It would be so easy to end it all.

I'm not talking about killing myself. I haven't the strength for that. Not for that, not for anything. Not to speak, not to walk, not to think, not to eat. Maybe not even to breathe. Stop doing everything. Because what is the point?

They make me do it every morning, go and face the day. But I don't know why. I'm an onlooker in my own life.

And all the time, this one question: *Is it our fault?*

I'd really like to be able to be angry with Joanne for asking this question. But I forced her to talk. I wanted it more than anything. Now I'm haunted by her words. They get louder and louder: *Is it really our fault?*

I can see Mathias's face. On the first day of fifth grade.

This September, when I gave him the brush-off. All the times he was laughed at.

And then I see his face at the moment when he turned the gun on me. So – cold. He was a different person. A Mathias Staudt that none of us had ever seen before.

These thoughts overwhelm me. And now I'm sitting with this woman, who is giving me the clear impression that she knows exactly what is going on in my head.

'What did you do today, Miriam?' she asks me.

What a stupid question! I sat all day next to a mute Joanne, keeping my eyes on the doors so that a murderer with a weapon couldn't creep into our classroom without anyone noticing. And after that I shouted at the grave of my dead boyfriend. What does this woman want me to say?

'You look very distressed, Miriam.'

Oh, really? Always these clever observations. And you actually get BLOODY paid for this kind of rubbish? No wonder there are so many psychologists. They talk nonsense all day and get good money for it.

'Have I told you before about the group therapy that is available to students of your school?'

I snarl, 'No, but that's fine.'

'Everyone is different. For some people, one-to-one therapy is better, others prefer group discussion. You can try both.' Dr Frei is giving me this penetrating look.

Does she want to get rid of me? I must have become a very depressing person if even my psychologist wants shut of me.

Group therapy. More chit-chat. That's the last thing I

need right now. She can stick her suggestions you-know-where.

'Tell me what you think of that?' She's giving me a cheery smile.

I can't describe exactly what is happening inside me. Suddenly there's this unbelievable anger. What she has said really makes me see red. There's a feeling of pressure in my stomach. My mouth pulls itself into a straight line, and before I know what I am doing, I start to shout at her. Words that I have suppressed for weeks come pouring out of my mouth, uncontrolled, unconsidered.

'I can tell you what I want, can I? So I'm allowed to have an opinion? I'm absolutely fed up with everyone telling me how I should behave. And the way you expect me to have an opinion on every bloody feeling! Nobody knows how I really am. NOT YOU, NOT ANYONE! SO SHUT UP! I JUST WANT A BIT OF PEACE.

I'm breathing fast. My chest is heaving. I'm like an onlooker at this moment. Surprised and relieved, I watch this girl shouting at her psychologist, her eyes wild, her face white as a sheet.

I watch as all the pressures of the past weeks come pouring out of the girl. The words are tumbling out faster and faster. 'Nobody accepts that I'm not the same any more. What did you expect? That I'd just go on the same as always? And then they get my *mother*. I CAN'T TAKE ANY MORE! My boyfriend was shot in front of me and I did nothing about it. I DIDN'T HELP HIM. My best friend won't talk. Sophia has turned into a junkie.

Tanja isn't here any more!!! School is hell. I'M AFRAID OF EVERYTHING!!!' My blue eyes stare in horror at Dr Frei. 'Mathias Staudt shot at me. His gun was pointed at me … I can't take any more …'

I bang the back of my head hard against the wall. The dull thud brings me back to myself. Shocked, I look at my shaking hands and then at my legs. I'm shaking all over. Why am I shaking?

Is it quiet in the room? I can't say. There's a roaring in my ears. Is it cold? My body is numb. There's a veil in front of my eyes, everything is blurred.

Is the world still spinning? I have expressed things that I was sure I had buried deep inside me, invisible to everyone.

'Yes, Miriam, you can.' Dr Freils voice seems to come from far away. 'You're doing really, really well. And it will get better.'

We are often afraid to express things because we think they could throw us into despair. That it will all lead to something terrible, because you can never take back what you've said. But in reality, that's not what happens.

Dr Frei hands me a glass of water. My outburst hasn't bothered her in the slightest.

'Better?' she asks gently.

To my own astonishment, I nod.

CHAPTER 11

I'm at Dr Frei's again. We're sitting in the comfortable armchairs, drinking fruit tea with a lot of sugar, lost in our thoughts. Or rather, I'm lost in my thoughts. Dr Frei is watching me.

I have an urge to talk to her. It doesn't make me angry any more. I'm sorry I was so angry about everything and everyone. I don't want to be angry any more. I just want some peace. Somehow. Shouting at her like that a few days ago has changed everything. My burden has lessened. I feel lighter. And not so alone. For the first time, I have a tiny bit of confidence in myself, that maybe I can make it. I open my mouth and then close it again.

Dr Frei has seen that. She gives me an encouraging smile. 'Yes, well, sometimes you just have to take the risk.

'Can I tell you something?'

'Of course.'

She gives me an affirming nod, and although I don't know this woman very long, I believe her.

'I was at Toby's grave.' I hesitate for a moment. Grief threatens to overwhelm me, but I swallow and go on talking, before I change my mind. 'I shouted at him. I accused him of stuff ... being, now ...'

I take a deep breath. Dr Frei doesn't interrupt, which I am very grateful for. 'In any case, I was so angry. With him, with everyone. And with Mathias Staudt ... But the one I am most angry with is myself. And I have no idea why I am behaving like this. Why I ignore my father and shout at Toby and am so nasty to my whole family. I don't want to be like that. I love them all.'

Dr Frei listens patiently. She doesn't interrupt me, and she doesn't comfort me when I start to cry. And then something occurs to me. I realise that I haven't cried since the day Mathias went berserk.

That makes everything worse and I cry even more. I cry about Toby and about my friends, who are alive but are still lost to me. I cry for me and all the others who have experienced what I experienced. And I cry because I can't bear it any longer.

Dr Frei waits until I've calmed down a little. She gives me a handkerchief. 'It's OK to be angry. Anger is a good beginning. It's a sign that you are working your way through what has happened. There's no need to be ashamed of it.'

I don't say anything. I'm still snivelling to myself, and Dr Frei lets me be. 'But at school, everyone is trying to pretend nothing happened, as if everything is fine, the way it always was.'

She purses her lips. 'That's understandable, I think.'

'You think so?'

'Everyone reacts differently to violence. But the easiest thing is not to engage with it. To behave as if you're fine. After all, you don't like to let other people know what's going on inside your head either, right?'

I give a laugh. It's not a nice laugh. It's mean, and somehow scary.

'It's none of their business.'

We say nothing for a moment. Then Dr Frei asks, 'Do you blame your boyfriend for dying?'

I think for a moment. 'I know, it sounds horrible, but sometimes I wish I could hate him for it. Then it wouldn't hurt so much.' I don't try to explain any more.

Dr Frei seems to understand anyway. She looks at me kindly and asks softly, 'So what was Toby like?'

I start to think about him and at exactly that moment I'm overcome by a mixture of grief and bliss. 'He was different from any other boy I ever knew. I only *really* saw him for the first time in Spain, in the summer. We did go to the same school, but we hadn't ever come across each other before …'

I am so angry.

Dad and I have flown to Spain to get away from it all and have a good time. But since we got here, his phone has been ringing every five minutes.

I'm stomping on the sand. It's very early in the morning,

only seven o'clock, and there's hardly anyone on the beach. Even though the sun is already up, I'm frozen in my skimpy shorts and white tunic. You can tell already that this day is going to be even hotter than the last two. I've braided my long blond hair into an untidy plait and I'm wearing big sunglasses.

As if it's not bad enough that someone has rung at *seven o'clock in the morning*, but then Dad has to go so far as to send me out of the room.

Angrily, I grab a shell and throw it into the sea, shouting out loud, 'Bloody place, bloody holiday!'

Startled, a couple of birds fly off.

'Hey, babe, if you made only half as much noise, other people could enjoy the beach.'

Irritated, I turn around to the voice that is making such a smart remark. It belongs to a boy who is sitting on a rock, looking down at me. He has brown hair and a tanned body. He's wearing only a pair of torn jeans. When he looks at me, I forget to breathe. He has such beautiful eyes. The most beautiful eyes I have ever seen.

I'm trying to think of something smart to say, but I just stutter, 'Hey, aren't we at the same school?'

He thinks for a moment. '9C?'

'And you? 10 ...?'

'10A,' he says helpfully. 'I'm Toby.'

'Miriam.'

Toby makes room for me on his rock and I sit beside him.

'Listen, I don't find Spain so bad. What's so bloody about it?' He uses the exact word I did and gives me a crooked grin. I can feel the blood rushing to my cheeks, and I look quickly out to sea, so that he won't notice.

'My dad threw me out of our hotel room because he has to work.' I roll my eyes and add, 'And it's been like this for days.'

'And you're going to let that ruin *your* holiday?'

It's not as simple as this boy seems to think. I explain that my dad's always working. I can't remember the last time he was really off. Officially, he does take his holidays. Only he's glued to his mobile all day, because there are always things to be dealt with. Work comes first.

'That's how it seems anyway.' I shrug.

Surprised, I look up as a hand appears in my field of vision. The hand takes my sunglasses off. I blink.

'We really should do something about that.' Toby gives me an impish grin.

I look back at him, amused. 'Are you taking advantage of my desperate situation?'

He jumps up, grabs my hand and pulls me along.

'What are you doing?'

'Making sure you don't ruin your holiday.'

We walk along together. My dad definitely wouldn't find it one bit funny if I go off with a strange boy. But he's busy.

'Where are we going? I haven't got a thing with me.'

'Doesn't matter. I'll show you the market.

'And there he sat, with his unbelievably sweet smile. And he made sure my holiday was fab, even though my father was working almost all the time.' My voice breaks and the stupid tears come again.

I take a deep breath and try to pull myself together.

'He left two days before me. He gave me his mobile number. The first thing I did when I got home was to ring Toby. And then it all developed between us. He always gave me a sense of security. Something I hadn't felt for a long time.'

And will never feel again.

'What would you say to him, if you could see him once?'

I don't need to think about that for long. 'That I love him. And that he gave me a feeling of being grounded in a world where I had felt unsure of myself. And, of course, that I miss him terribly.'

'So say it to him.'

'How?'

'Write it down. You can write Toby a letter. That's like a formal farewell for you.'

But this farewell means accepting that I will never see someone ever again ...

I whisper softly, 'But if I don't want to say goodbye?'

CHAPTER 12

Do you know those nights, when you are totally exhausted but you can't get to sleep? When you toss and turn, feel hot and then cold. When you're afraid of the dark and so you turn on the light, and then you turn it off because it's too bright and it gives you a headache. Do you know those nights in which you long for the morning, but at the same time, you fear nothing so much as the morning.

That's the kind of night I'm having. The conversation with Dr Frei made me agitated. On the one hand, I feel better, because I've expressed so much. But on the other hand, I'm aware that I'm always going to have this weight on my soul, something I can't tell anyone about.

I keep thinking about Toby and the holiday in Spain. And about the two days I spent on my own because he left before me. God, I thought those two days would never be over. I just wanted to get on the next aeroplane and fly back immediately to Germany.

I take my mobile off the bedside table and press the number 2. I know now that it takes exactly sixteen seconds for his Voicemail to start up. Then come the sentences that I know by heart by now: 'Hi. It's Toby. I can't answer my mobile right now. But don't bother to leave a message. I never listen to my voicemail.'

I hang up and immediately press the speed dial number again. It takes another sixteen seconds, then I hear his voice again. My lips form the words soundlessly as he says them.

Ever since that time I cried in Dr Frei's office, tears come all the time. I can't stop. My finger keeps pressing the number 2 automatically. Until I notice Toby's voice at the edge of my consciousness. It's like an addiction. I can't stop.

I keep hearing his jokey voice. It's so sad that that these sentences are all that I can hear of him. These three sentences for the rest of my life. No more *I love you*. No laughter. Just three stupid sentences recorded on a voicemail.

At some point I stop dialling his number. I let the mobile fall onto my quilt. I stare out into the night and wish I could see the stars. But they are hidden behind the clouds. If only it would snow! But the fat red clouds just hang there in the sky, blocking my view of the stars.

Suddenly I think of a song. 'Life without you' by Stabfour. I always liked that song. But I didn't know how close it would come to reality.

I sigh and turn onto my back. Can you die of loneliness? I bet you can. I've never felt so alone in my whole life. Toby is gone. Joanne can't be reached. I'm alone.

I feel hot. I push the covers back. Then I turn on my side. I can see the outline of my room. Part of me doesn't want to go to sleep, because I can't stand the nightmares any more. But another part longs for rest, because I feel so exhausted and empty.

The day Mathias went berserk keeps playing in my head. I should let it go, but I can't. I think about that sentence. The only sentence that Joanne has addressed to me since that day.

Is it our fault?

We were nasty to Mathias. But that is no reason to do something like that to us.

Is it our fault?

Something comes back to me. Something I'd almost forgotten. It was a while ago. Toby and I had just got together. We both forgot about it afterwards. But Mathias never forgot it.

'Oh, stop it.'

Toby has put an arm around my waist and he's tickling me. He laughs and I snuggle more closely in to him. We're wandering around town. It's summer and I'm wearing a short summer dress and I have my big sunglasses on again. Toby's wearing check shorts and a white printed T-shirt. He's wearing his pilot's sunglasses.

I'm aware that we're an attractive couple. He's tall, sun-tanned, with light brown hair and deep green eyes.

I'm dark blond with midnight-blue eyes. I'm just a head shorter than him and my feminine curves are perfect with his muscled torso. We look great together. Everyone turns around to look at us.

I have a super life. I'm loved. Have the perfect boyfriend, the best girlfriends in the world. I haven't got a mother who gives me grief, like Joanne. I feel wonderful, and I show that to everyone with a smile as big as the sun.

Toby and I are planning to go for an ice-cream and then we'll go to the park. We'll lie on the grass, chat, snog. We'll definitely snog.

'Joanne was so cross. You know, pretending to be cross. Really she's delighted for us.'

Toby smiles and presses a kiss into my hair. 'Do you know? One of my pals is mad about her. We could play Cupid and organise a date. Or we could do a double-date, to set the others up.'

'Sure. Who is it?'

Toby is just about to answer when a boy comes running right up to me. I stagger backwards and of course I bang my ankle. It starts pounding immediately. That's just great. It'll definitely go a nice shade of blue and green and yellow.

'Oh ... sorry. I ... I mean, I didn't see you. Sor ... I mean ...'

'Hey, man, can't you watch where you're going? You've just hurt my girlfriend!'

I look up. The boy who has banged into me is Mathias Staudt. A loser from my school who is always hiding in the boys' toilet on the first floor with his two loser friends.

Toby holds out his hand and pulls me up. It hurts to put my weight on my foot.

'Well, you made a good job of that. My ankle is definitely twisted. Can you tell me how I am supposed to get home?'

'Ah … my mother could maybe … Her car …'

'Your mummy?' asks Toby contemptuously. 'Forget it. I'd rather *carry* Miriam home. She'd get a shock if it stinks in your car as badly as you do. Have you ever heard of a shower? Or deodorant? That'd help.'

I snort. It's getting silly. 'Come on, Toby, let's go. There's no point in this.'

We just go, and leave a stammering Mathias behind. I'm cross with Staudt. He's ruined our lovely afternoon. Instead, Toby and I have to go home and strap up my foot. Fantastic. Really. People like Mathias Staudt should go to a special school for disturbed kids. What a creep!

Joanne's question won't go away.

Is it our fault?

But I don't allow myself to think about it. I'm not going to look for the answer, because I'm afraid of it. I'm so afraid of it.

Is it our fault?

I pull the covers back up, because I'm cold. It doesn't matter what I do. It doesn't matter what I think. It's always going to hurt. I'm always going to be reminded of what I have lost and what I can never have again. Doesn't matter whether I eat or study or read, I'll never be able to forget. It'll go on dogging me like a shadow.

I can't even say if it matters whose fault it was. Because whether it's this or that isn't going to change anything. I'll never be able to forget it. Same as all the others who were at school that day. But the thing I can least forget is that question.

I'm hot again, and I let my legs hang out of my bed. Then I turn onto my stomach. I take a deep breath and as I breathe out, I imagine I'm breathing out all my memories and feelings.

In my dream, I'm alone. All around me are mirrors. Right, left, above, below, in front, behind. I'm imprisoned in a little room made of mirrors.

Only the room doesn't seem small because everything is endlessly reflected. In my dream, I still have long blond hair and I'm wearing a long white dress. My eyes are wide with fright. I feel I can't breathe in the room and I beat against the mirrors. But it doesn't matter how much strength I use, I can't get out.

I get really panicked, desperate for air. Then one of my reflections moves. It wavers in front of me and says, 'So, Miriam, what's all this about? Are you still trying to convince yourself that you are an innocent little girl? We both know better than that.'

And with these words, it pulls the long hair from my head and my new short red hair is left.

I turn away, scared. But there's another reflection waiting for me. It's grinning just as evilly as the first and starts to pull at my dress.

'What's all this, Miriam? White? That's the colour of purity. I think this colour suits you better.' With one yank, she pulls the white dress off my body, leaving a black dress behind. The black material is sticking to my body and it feels so horrible that I want to pull it off. But it doesn't matter how hard I pull, the dress clings to me.

I sink to the ground and hide my face in the black material. I tuck it in around my legs and start to cry.

A sound startles me. The noise echoes, although the room is so small. It's a clicking sound. The kind of click that only happens when you load a gun.

Shaking, I look up. My heart contracts when I see the infinite reflections, each one pointing a gun at me.

When they shoot, every single bullet hits me. The mirrors shatters into thousands of tiny shards. They tinkle to the ground and sink into my blood.

'Good morning. How did you sleep?'

I answer my father's question with a grunt. Listlessly, I get a yoghurt out of the fridge and start to stir it. I am not one bit hungry.

'That bad?'

I have to hand it to him: he is very attentive. Much more than before. But that doesn't dispel the dreams and the loneliness.

'You don't look well. Maybe we should go to the doctor?'

I push his hand away, annoyed. 'And what's he going to do? He'll tell us I'm not sleeping well and have a few psychological problems.'

Dad makes a pained face.

OK, so I don't make it easy for him. But I have no interest in company, small-talk or visits to the doctor. I hate going to the doctor. You sit for two hours in the waiting room, pick up some bug or other from strangers, and then you spend eleven minutes in a stinking surgery and then you get sent home without it having done any good.

'Really, Dad,' I add. 'A doctor can't help me. We have to do that ourselves.'

'But I don't want to stand idly by while you are suffering. Maybe you should make another appointment with Dr Frei?'

To set his mind at rest, I say, 'OK. I'll ask her.'

He nods. He doesn't look too convinced, but it calms him down.

Because I know for sure that I'll feel terrible later if I don't eat anything now, I make myself swallow the yoghurt. Then I grab my bag and go to school.

Sophia is outside the school building, smoking. I speed

up, so I can get past her quickly, but Sophia takes hold of my arm and pulls me towards her.

She blows disgusting smoke into my face and laughs. 'Miriam, loosen up. Take a look at yourself. Your eyes are sunk in your head, black rings around them. Tut-tut.' She shakes her head in mock shock.

I raise an eyebrow at her, wondering if she means it. After all, she is the one that stinks to high heaven, wears the same clothes all week and has bad breath. 'I could say the same to you. Have you ever heard of soap?'

Sophia laughs as if it is a great joke. I am starting to doubt if Sophia is able to take anything seriously. Maybe she's too high for that.

'You think I'm a stinking dope-head,' she says, suddenly dead serious. She's right. That's exactly what I think. She shakes her head sadly. 'Better than a disturbed psycho like Joanne or a grieving bundle of nerves like you. Do you know, my way is much easier. And more fun.'

'You're ruining your life.'

Sophia laughs again. It's beginning to frighten me. 'Are you serious? Look around you, Miriam. Our lives have already been ruined. All I'm doing is trying to keep it as far away from me as possible. Give it a try. It's much easier my way.'

It sounds so attractive that I don't know what I'd have done if Vanessa hadn't appeared at that moment. She takes my arm and says to Sophia, 'Destroy yourself if you want to, girl, but count us out.'

Vanessa pulls me along. Sophia is still laughing and she calls after me, 'You know how to find me.'

'Definitely not,' murmurs Vanessa.

We go into the classroom and sit on the window-seat.

Vanessa shakes her head. 'You and I are the only ones out of the five of us who are half normal. I don't for a moment believe you are going to let Sophia drag you into *that*.'

'But she's right,' I say. 'Our lives are in tatters.'

Vanessa pushes my hair back, like she used to do. 'And we're still going downhill.'

'Sophia too?'

Vanessa thinks for a while. 'She could be getting into a relationship with Jan.'

'Eeek!' I shriek, and for just one moment things are the way they used to be. It wouldn't take much for me and Vanessa to start laughing.

The bell rings for class and we sit at our desks. Joanne sits next to me. I'm really worried about her. Sophia is right. Joanne is a psycho. By comparison with her, I'm relaxed and balanced. I'd like to ask her how she is, but it's like talking to the wall.

I'm dying for the spring. For the warmth of the sun, flowers in blossom, green trees, birds singing. I long for strawberries, butterflies and babbling brooks. I long for a bit of warmth. Who knows, it might even melt the ice in my heart.

The first two classes go by. I can't really follow the

lessons. My thoughts are still with Sophia and Joanne. My best friends. What has become of them?

At break, Vanessa and I sit outside in the yard, freezing. We don't say much. And when we do speak, it's only about lessons. I'm delighted when the bell rings. We have a free period. I sit in the canteen (also only a container, of course) and do my homework. Vanessa sits down beside me, takes out her exercise books.

'Do you know what I look forward to most about leaving school?'

I shake my head.

'No more Latin. It's really a terrible language. Who on earth thought it up? And it's supposed to be such a logical language. Absolutely logical that there are a thousand exceptions to the rules.' She shakes her head.

I really have to give a little smile. Vanessa has been making this speech for ever.

'You're the one saying that? You only ever get As and Bs.'

Vanessa nods, 'Yes, and I know what I'd like to do with them. School is torture, but I'll get through it. And then I'm going to be a doctor.'

I give her a quizzical look. Am I supposed to be surprised? We always knew that Vanessa, who *understands*, has a bit of a helping complex.

'And then I'm going to Afghanistan.'

I almost choke. 'What?' I manage to say. 'Don't you think that's a bit extreme?'

'Think about it, Miriam. The children there have experienced worse things even than us. They've lost their parents and siblings, their homes. They are seriously ill or wounded. I want to help them, do you understand?'

I nod, but I don't think I really do understand. Vanessa wants to go, of her own free will, into a warzone and help the people there, because they are worse off than we are. I've never really thought much about other people. Or not since the shooting. I spend all my time feeling sorry for myself. I tell myself that nobody can understand me. I bend over my exercise book and say no more.

But Vanessa's plan won't leave me alone. In history and English, I can think of nothing else. Then I pack up my things and go.

At the door, a girl pushes past me. Out of the corner of my eye I see black hair, dark skin. Surprised, I look up. The girl used to be Philip Schwarz's girlfriend.

Images flash in front of my eyes. Shadows that can be seen from under the door of a toilet cubicle. The smell of gunshot, mixed with the filthy smell of school toilets. A dull thud.

I lower my eyes, ashamed. I can't look her in the eye. I don't even know this girl's name. But we have something in common. Our boyfriends. Our dead boyfriends. Both shot by Matthias Staudt. We both have to come to terms with that. She understands me better than anyone else.

But even she didn't see what I saw. What would she say if she knew that I did nothing to save her boyfriend. How would she react? Surely she wouldn't understand. She'd put the blame on me.

I wish I could turn the clock back, so I could do things differently. But now it's too late. She must never find out. Nobody must ever find out.

CHAPTER 13

There's nothing but crap on television. That's one thing my mum and I can agree on anyway. She turns it off in disgust. 'Why do we have a damn goggle-box at all?'

I shrug. 'So we can watch boring courtroom dramas and home-grown series about hospitals.'

My mother shakes her head. 'If we have to watch hospital programmes, then at least it should be *Gray's Anatomy*.'

I nod in agreement. She gives me a strange look. 'Has something happened. You seem so ...' She searches for words. 'You haven't used a single swear-word to me today. Not that I mind, but it's almost worrying. Your dad tells me you had another nightmare.'

Normally, I would turn away from her angrily and run to my room, because I don't like it when my father discusses me with her, as if we were still a family. But I'm confused and could do with advice from an adult. Even from my mother, if there's nobody else.

'I'm worried about Joanne, my best friend.' I add the last bit, because I'm not sure if Mum knows who Joanne is.

'Why?'

'She's … she's been behaving very strangely since … the shooting. She doesn't talk to anyone any more. Not even the teachers. She's like an empty husk.'

'Is she getting help?' Mum asks carefully, and with more understanding than I'd have believed her capable of.

'I don't know. I can't imagine it, with that mother she has. She's pretty difficult. But I can't stop thinking about going to talk to her about Joanne.'

'More difficult than me? Hardly possible.' Mum gives me a conspiratorial wink.

I force a smile, though I don't find the joke funny. All the same, she's trying to help me. That's new for both of us.

'She's different from you … Mum.' I'm trying out how this name feels on my tongue. I haven't used it for ages. Mum touches me on the shoulder. And, although I usually try to avoid all contact with her, today I like it. It even helps. 'If you like, I can drive you over there tomorrow. We can both speak to her.'

I nod and lay my head on her shoulder, something I would never have done before. But today I haven't the strength for fighting. And anyway, it feels very good. Safe, secure. That I could feel like this about my mum is something I'd never have dreamt.

'Has anyone said to you how fantastically you're doing?'

'Yeah, sure,' I answer her ironically.

'No, really, you're doing fantastically. I admire you, the way you're trying to get on with your life. Sometimes I look at you and I wonder how parents like us could have produced such a wonderful girl.'

I want to contradict her, because I know that she's not right. Maybe I could say it to Mum, tell her how it really was, that I behaved horribly, just like Toby and lots of others. But I don't. I don't want to break the mood. So I just snuggle in to her and enjoy this feeling as long as it lasts.

Mum's kept her promise. We're outside Joanne's door. We drove here immediately after school. We've agreed that I will speak first, and Mum will come in if Joanne's mother refuses to listen. And believe me, she'll do that. She won't be able to bear to hear that Joanne is not perfect.

'Ready?' asks my mother.

'Not one bit,' I reply. Then we ring the bell. My heart is in my mouth. After a few seconds, the door opens. It's Dana, Joanne's mother. She looks tired, exhausted.

'Miriam.' She sounds surprised. 'Eh … I'm sorry, but I don't think Joanne is in any condition to see you. She's really not well.'

She is visibly uneasy. I can understand that. I don't feel all that different myself. Only Mum seems not to find the situation strange. A few weeks ago, I used to ring at this door all the time. Now it seems peculiar. How quickly habits can change!

'Hello, Dana. I don't want to see Joanne. It's you I wanted to speak to.' Noticing her wary look, I add, 'This is my mum, by the way.'

'Miriam's mother,' Dana mutters to herself. Then she puts out a hand and shakes Mum's. 'I never expected to meet you,' she says, eyeing Mum's piercings and tattoos suspiciously.

Then she stands aside, so that Mum and I can enter the apartment. It looks the same in there as always. White carpets, smart furniture, all eerily tidy. Not as much as a magazine lying around. Every object has its place, and it's in its place too. Only two years ago, Dana had the place done up and bought new furniture. All designer stuff, of course. Joanne and I joked about it for weeks.

We sit down in the living room.

'Would you like something to drink? Tea, coffee, water?'

I shake my head and Mum also refuses politely. I have no idea how my mother is going to make it clear to Dana, as sensibly and as carefully as possible, that her daughter has mutated into a psycho.

'I'd like to talk to you about Joanne,' I begin. 'I'm worried about her.'

'Has she spoken to you? Has she said anything to you?' asks Dana.

I shake my head again. 'No, not really.' I think about

that one sentence. But I can't really call that a conversation. 'She doesn't talk to me any more.'

Dana covers her face briefly with her hands. 'I know that she's very closed at the moment. But I imagine that lots of the kids at school are the same. She's going through a very difficult phase.'

That's so typical of Dana. 'It's not a phase, Dana. Hardly anyone at school is as bad as Joanne. I'm really worried.'

'She just needs time to get over it.'

'Under normal circumstances, I'd agree with you. But I am watching Joanne getting worse and worse every day. She's getting paler all the time. All the time. And more lifeless, to the point that it's almost impossible.'

I fold my arms. To be here, in this room, brings back too many memories. It hurts.

Dana gives me a hostile look. But in her eyes I can see something else. Fear. Fear of losing control.

'We're doing fine. Thank you for your visit.'

We couldn't be more politely dismissed, but I'm not going to be so easily got rid of. Mum sees it the same way, because now she puts in her oar. 'Dana, we don't want to upset you, but Joanne needs help. Professional help.'

'Who are you to say that? Where were you all those times that Miriam came here to eat with us after school?'

Mum doesn't deserve accusations like this. She's really stood by me today.

'This is not about my mother. Joanne needs your help. She can't get through this on her own. None of us can.'

I brace my shoulders and go to the door. That was that. I don't know how I can support Joanne now. I can't do any more. It's not fair, but that's how it is. At least she behaved half normally to Mathias. She even gave me a piece of her mind when I went too far.

Joanne sits beside me on the table-tennis table and gives me a slantways look. 'So, tell me, what's wrong?'

I don't want to talk about it. I'd like to just forget this whole stupid thing. But my best friend isn't going to be satisfied with that. She's going to pester me about this blasted thing for days. So I may as well tell her at once.

'Mathias Staudt has just asked me if I would like to go to the ball with him.' I roll my eyes and laugh. Though really I don't much feel like laughing. I don't want Tanja and Joanne to know that my conscience is pricking me.

'What?' Tanja laughs too and rolls onto her stomach, so that she can look at us. 'What did you say to that?'

'What a stupid question!' Joanne jokes. 'Miriam undoubtedly announced her undying love and is now wondering what kind of a dress she will wear.'

I giggle, and give Joanne a friendly dig in the ribs with my elbow. Then I shake my head and say, 'I told him I'd rather go to a ball by myself than with him.'

Tanja laughs again. 'If he only knew what you and

Toby are really planning for that evening.' She gives me a knowing wink.

'I didn't tell him that.'

Tanja pulls a face, and I add. 'But I did tell him that he's a pig and stinks like one too. Oh, yes, and that he should wash his hair. And I told him I wouldn't want to go out with him if he were the lasts boy on earth.'

I feel better about it, having told the others the story. It doesn't seem so wrong, when we can laugh about it. But then I realise that Joanne isn't laughing any more.

'That bit about being a pig and the smell – you could have left that out. That's downright mean. It cost him a lot to ask you.'

I know myself that that was a blow below the belt. But Joanne's reproof needles me, because now I feel really guilty. It's none of her business.

'Come on. You and I have often laughed about him.'

She gives me a sad, disappointed look. 'Exactly. We laughed *about* him. But now you've really insulted him. There's a difference. If we're mean about him at home in my house, at least he can't hear us.'

I can't quite grasp that my best friend can say such a thing to me. She's supposed to stand up for me, whatever I say or do. I feel I've been cornered by her.

'Toby and his mates do a lot of mean things,' I say in my own defence.

'What's your problem, Joanne?' Tanja butts in.

'My problem is,' says Joanne, 'that you'd never have said

a thing like that before. Not like that. You're right. Toby does very mean things!' She takes a deep breath and tries to calm herself. 'But that doesn't make it right that you copy your boyfriend. Just because he behaves stupidly is no reason why you should.'

I snort and fold my arms. That's just great. It's not bad enough that I should have a bad conscience about it, but now Joanne has to add in her tuppence-worth as well. And the worst of it is that, somehow, she's right.

CHAPTER 14

I can't remember when I was last in church before the memorial service. I think it was with Grandma, but I'm not sure. The answer to when I last prayed is easy. Never. (Because I don't think the few times I did it as a child count. I didn't even know then what praying was.)

I can't say what on earth I'm doing in a church now. But here I am and have no idea how to behave.

There are people who find answers when they pray. There are people who find answers by reading. There are people who find answers by dreaming. There are people who find answers by going for a walk. There are people who find answers by jogging. There are people who find answers all by themselves. And there are people who find answers only when they are surrounded by people. And there are people who do not find answers. I'm one of those.

Lots of old people go to church because they believe that God will forgive them their sins. Because they know they will die soon, only have a few years left. I believe they're there to find refuge in God. Because nobody does nothing but good in their life. Everyone has something that they regret. And when you get old and realise that death could come at any moment, then you think about your mistakes.

But God can't forgive sins. The only one who can do that is yourself. You have to forgive yourself for what you have done. You're the one who has to live with it your whole life long.

At the end of the day, those who have always tried to live well and justly blame themselves, and those who were mean and egotistical live happily until the very last second.

I sit at the very back of the church and look around. The frescoes, the paintings, the sculptures. I admire the beautifully decorated church.

In the old days, I used to find churches scary. They seemed so mighty and old. And it was always so quiet in church.

I've never understood why you are supposed to be quiet in church. While I'm sitting here, I think of something I read once somewhere. *When candles burn, the stillness of our souls is revealed.* That's true. And I find the stillness of my soul here in a place that is really alien to me.

I stay sitting for a while. I'm doing nothing. Not even thinking. Just … being.

Then I stand up and go to the door. I almost bump into an old man. He has a pile of flyers under his arm and a pair of glasses on his nose. He gives me a friendly smile. Which makes lots of little laughter-lines appear around his eyes.

'Oops-a-daisy, miss. Not so fast.'

I smile back automatically. 'Sorry.'

He lets me pass and I go to the place that I desperately want to avoid but at the same time need. To the cemetery, to Toby's grave.

I sit on the ground by his grave, without giving a thought to the cold. That's another thing I'd never have done before. I wouldn't have wanted to dirty my clothes.

Such irrelevancies are not important to me today, but everything has got much more complicated. If I could, I'd change in a flash back into the superficial cow I used to be.

Would Toby love the girl I am today? And would I love him, if he were alive? Probably our relationship would have broken up, like my friendship with Joanne and Tanja.

There is such a big hole in my heart. I'd like to be able to laugh again. And sing. And feel secure again. How great it would be to be able to look in the mirror and not despise myself or feel sorry for myself.

I can't exactly explain what happened today in church. I don't believe in the church. Not even a little. Perhaps there is something out there that is more powerful than us all. But for me, it's certainly not the church. In my opinion, the church was created by humans and therefore it's fallible.

So it's not faith that's had this effect on me. It was something else. The church was … quiet. It exuded a peace that I haven't experienced in a long time. I felt whole and not shattered into a thousand pieces.

I spend hours sitting on the floor, staring at the photo album. But I'm not even looking properly at the photos. I'm just sitting there. Dr Frei says that's OK. I should do anything that feels OK to me. I've forgotten what it feels like to do things that are just OK.

There's a knock on my door. To my surprise, it's my mother, holding a tray in her hands. She gives me a cautious smile. When she stands there like that, wearing just a tracksuit, not weighed down with piercings and covered in makeup, she looks quite pretty. Like before. Before she left.

'You should eat something.'

There's a bowl of noodle soup and a glass of cola on the tray. She puts it down carefully on my bed and sits down beside it. I give her a surprised stare. It's years since she made soup for me. So long ago that I can't even remember it. The soup tastes of childhood. Of security. Of a time when I still had a lovely life.

'Thanks,' is all I say. There is so much more to say.

Some day I'll tell her how I felt that morning when she was just gone. How much she disappointed me.

'If you could turn back the clock and undo things, would you do it?' I ask her.

She doesn't think long. 'I've often asked myself the same question. But then I gave up on it, because it didn't get me anywhere.' She stays silent for a moment and tucks my short red hair behind my ear. I get the feeling she likes it.

'We can't undo things. And even if we could, we shouldn't. Because everything has a point, however mad that sounds.'

Mum strokes my forehead. Which is frowning, and she continues. 'Of course the first months and years were hard. And I'm not proud that I threw myself at one man after another. I did it because I was looking for love, but I didn't find it that way. I was very young when I became pregnant. I know I'm not a model mother. I realise that. It's OK if you are cross about my leaving you. I had my reasons, of course. I had never imagined a life like that. I wanted to see the world. But I am the mother and you are the child. I was wrong. You have every right to hold that against me. But even so, I hope you can find a place for me in your life. Some time anyway.'

I spoon up a bit more soup and offer it to her. With a smile, she opens her mouth and I feed her. When did we last sit together in peace like this? Not before the shooting.

'On the other hand, I've seen the world. I fulfilled my dearest wish. I'd given that up when I married your father. Do me a favour and never get married just because you are pregnant. I still love your father in a way, after all these years. How could I not? After all, he is the father of my daughter.' She kisses me on the forehead. 'Neither of us is cut out for marriage. But in the past few weeks, a friendship has developed between us that is worth a thousand times more to me than our previous relationship.'

I have to think about this. It's true, my mother has travelled all over the world. She was in Madagascar, Zambia, Russia and Egypt. She has seen the Eiffel Tower, the Leaning Tower of Pisa, the Great Wall of China, Niagara Falls and the Statue of Liberty. But she has paid a very high price for it all.

'I think I can balance good and bad in life. You have to work to make that happen. You can't ever give up.'

She must have noticed my dubious look, because she asks, 'When I left you, what nice things happened after that?'

'My girls. Vanessa, Sophia, Joanne and Tanja are the best girlfriends you could wish for. And after that came Toby.' Just to mention his name hurts. A single tear runs down my face.

'Look.' She wipes the tear away and lifts my chin so that I am looking right at her. 'I promise you, this time you'll find something new too. That is the eternal journey of life. Winning and losing. Give and take. Nobody has it good all the time.'

'But there are people who will never experience good times again.' I shouldn't say that, but it just slips out. Mum knows I'm right. There are people who never recover from a blow like this. People like Joanne. She'll probably never be normal again.

'You'll make it.'

My mother's voice is full of confidence. I wish I could believe her. But I can't believe that the feelings I am having now could ever make way for anything else.

'How come you're so sure about that?'

I take the last spoon of soup. It's as if the last of the past that it represents disappears.

My mother looks at me steadily, confidently. I've never noticed before how lovely her eyes are. I've never seen eyes that are at the same time so light and so brown.

'You've experience so much already. Almost too much for your age. But you've matured through it. Even if you and your dad aren't aware of it, you've already taken a huge step forward. And even though he is concerned about you, I think we should trust you. You'll need time, but you can have that. And at some stage you'll get up and find you have recovered your enthusiasm for life. You'll be able to smile again. I don't just *think* you'll make it. I *know* you'll make it.'

She stands up, takes the tray in her hand and leans forward to kiss my hair. A gesture that I wouldn't have tolerated before. 'Bad memories about the past never completely disappear. But we forget them in our happiest moments. And you, sweetheart, have a lot of those moments ahead of you.'

My mother's words are occupying my thoughts. She seems to be so sure. So sure that I'll take the right path. But I have no idea where this path is to be found. Never mind where it is going to take me. I envy Mum her optimism.

Something has changed between us. I can feel it. She's supporting me. I accept her help. But sooner or later, my mum will leave again, because when she stays in one place for a long time, she feels like a caged bird. She needs freedom and adventure and she won't find that here.

When she goes, I'll miss her again, just like before, when I was a child.

I don't love her the way I did before. Now it's more like a friendship that links us, but in the past few weeks I've learnt how much it hurts to lose a friend.

Girlfriends are important. And it doesn't look as if I have too many of them.

I comb my hair and clean my teeth. I give myself plenty of time. I try to concentrate on everyday things. Another of those things that Dr Frei has advised me to do. Before I go back into my room, I give myself a few more minutes. I lean on the washbasin, close my eyes and just breathe.

Breathe in, breathe out, breathe in, breathe out. Even that seems difficult. I have to relearn everything. I try to start with simple things. Like breathing.

Perhaps Mum is right. Perhaps I'll feel better one day. But, if that's so, I'll need a lot of strength and a lot of time to get there. I'll need weeks, months and years. Maybe even my whole life.

I knew it. I can't sleep. I'm not even trying. I get into bed, snuggle down in my nest of covers and pillows, and hug Bella hard. Bella used to be my favourite soft toy. A pink pig. A few years ago, I threw her out, because I thought I was too old for a thing like that. But now Dad has put her back in my bed. When I hug Bella, I remember the good times. She calms me, because she is a sign that nobody can take my happy memories from me. They'll stay with me.

I toss and turn for hours. I'm hot and cold at the same time. I'm totally over-tired. At the end, half of my body is covered, the other half not. So I'm freezing and sweating about equally.

My eyelids are heavy. I'm so tired. But healing sleep won't come. I keep drifting off, but I don't really sleep. My eyes are closed. I lose track of time. But even so, I'm still aware of everything.

At some stage, I can't say whether it's after half an hour or after three hours, I give up. Tonight I won't be dreaming.

I go into the kitchen and make myself a hot chocolate. I turn on the radio and hum along to the melody of 'Billy Talent'.

I leave the light off. It's nice just to sit in the dark, drinking chocolate and listening to music. I glance at my mobile, which is lying on the kitchen counter.

I'm a hopeless case. I keep ringing my dead boyfriend's voicemail. That is so senseless. I should stop. I should say goodbye to him.

But instead of that, I ring his number and wait until the connection is made between the two networks. Then it rings, but the sound is different. Three high-pitched tones. Then a computerised voice says, 'There is no connection to this number.'

The telephone slips out of my hand and falls to the floor. The battery rattles out of it and slithers across the kitchen tiles.

There is no connection to this number. No, that can't be. Where is his voice gone? Where are those three stupid sentences that I've listened to a hundred times?

I put my hands to my face, force myself to think it through. It's so final. His family has de-registered his mobile. Because he doesn't need it any more. Because he's dead.

Toby has gone. For ever.

I never had a chance to say goodbye. Everything happened too quickly. I can't even remember when we last spoke to each other.

I think of Dr Frei's suggestion. It's the only way to say goodbye to him.

I tear a page out of my notepad and start writing.

CHAPTER 15

The snow melts. The sun comes out, the birds are twittering, and you can tell it's going to be spring soon.

All the same, I'm sad. Sad, because I know that life is going on all around me. And I keep experiencing that day over and over again in my head. I keep thinking back over my whole life.

Has it all been one big lie?

All those superficial activities, like shopping and going to parties, what have they led to. Apart from conflict with Toby, because I thought he drank too much. Apart from problems with Dad because I spent too much on shoes. Apart from discussions with Joanne because she bought tops that I wanted to have.

It cost me time. Valuable time that I could have spent in better pursuits. All I ever wanted to be was grown-up. Well, not really grown-up. Then you have so many responsibilities. But maybe twenty-one, twenty-two, that is a great age, I always thought. You have your own flat, but not many obligations. And as well as that, you don't have to go to school any more.

It never bothered me that I was losing my childhood. Until now. Until this decisive experience. I'd do anything to be as carefree as I was then. I could just lie in the grass and let the warm summer sun shine on me, playing with my stuffed toys.

I stare sadly at Toby's grave. I can't really describe what I feel. It's a kind of clenching in the chest, a lurching in the stomach. I miss him so much. I try not to think about that moment when I decided to save my life and not his.

It follows me like a shadow. Right now, I could do with having Toby around. His shoulder to lean on. His warm lips. His lovely eyes, twinkling sometimes with fun, sometimes with tenderness. All I want is someone who understands. There is only one person who saw what I saw. Joanne. But Joanne is an empty shell.

Something brushes my eyelid and I look up. It's beginning to rain. Big fat drops are falling from the sky and, in the distance, I can see a flash of lightning ripping through the air.

Well that's just great. That's all I needed. I make a dash for the church and go inside. Glimmering candlelight greets me. I sit down on the back pew and enjoy the silence.

I watch the candles, their flames flickering back and forth. I listen to the wind, which is sweeping over the treetops. I feel the cold of the old walls.

The creak of a door breaks the silence, drags me out of my thoughts. Startled, I turn around. My heart is racing.

Since the shooting, I have problems if I don't know exactly who is in a room with me.

In the doorway stands the older man that I almost bumped into a few days ago. He is soaking wet. When he shuts the wooden door, the sound echoes in the stillness. The old man smiles when he sees me.

'The church is a good place to seek comfort and sanctuary.'

'I'm only here because of the rain. Not because of God or any rubbish like that,' I hear myself saying. It slipped out, before I had a chance to think about it.

The man approaches me and nods towards the pew that I'm sitting on. 'May I?'

I shrug my shoulders. It's all the same to me what he does. As far as I am concerned, he can sit wherever he likes. But I want him to leave me alone. I don't want to talk. I just want to stare into space.

'It's so peaceful here. All your problems and worries seem much smaller.'

'So you must have a lot of problems, considering how often you are here?' I say it without thinking.

But luckily it doesn't seem to bother the man. He gives a friendly nod.

'Yes, I've been coming here for almost twenty years, since my wife died. At first, because I didn't know where to go with my sorrow. And afterwards, because playing the organ brings me such joy.'

'I don't think I'm going to start playing the organ, just because I'm sitting here.'

The man laughs softly. 'Nobody is going to make you do that. Not everyone responds to music.'

'I love music,' I protest. Then, more calmly, I add, 'Listening to music helps me. Then I don't feel so alone.'

He is still smiling. 'Is that why you are here?' I can see in his eyes what he doesn't say out loud: *Because you are lonely.*

I look at him in surprise for a moment. He's rumbled me. That's a good question. But I don't want to think about that. So I say sharply, 'Do I need a reason to be here?'

'There's a reason for everything. You're not here to pray, you don't play the organ. So then why are you here?'

'For the peace,' I say, once more without thinking. But it's the truth. 'I like the quiet.'

For the first time, I'm taking the time to consider what the man is saying. He's really very nice and on top of that, we have something in common. We have both lost someone we love.

'How did your wife die?'

'Brigitte had cancer. She died in her early forties. Far too early. She had so much still ahead of her. She never saw her children growing up.' There's something indescribably painful in the man's voice. I understand him. Better, perhaps, than he thinks.

'My boyfriend died at sixteen.' I stare at the altar as

I say it. I don't want to see the sympathy in his eyes. 'In that shooting this winter. I was there too. I was lucky.' I continue to examine the altar minutely. 'If you can call it luck to survive a thing like that.' It's the first time I've told a stranger about it.

'It's always better to survive than to die.'

I raise my eyebrows doubtfully. 'Is it?' I can hardly keep the tears back. I bite my lip hard. 'It doesn't feel like it.'

'I know that a maxim like that may not always help, but sometimes there is a spark of truth in such a saying. There is a lot of suffering in life. But that is not a reason to give up.'

Well, he would know. To lose his wife, to have to watch his children suffering too. All the same, I give him a sideways look. 'You're right. Mottos like that don't help.'

'I understand.' He shakes his head, smiles gently. 'My brother said something like that to me a few weeks after Brigitte's death. I asked him to leave, pretty rudely.' The man winks at me. 'I never could abide him.'

I laugh. The sound echoes around the old church. I listen in surprise. I don't think I laugh much any more. Before, I was always doing it. Now it sounds weird to my ears. Sometimes I let out rough, jokey sounds that approach laughter, but I haven't given a proper, joyful laugh for a long time.

I look at the man again. Although he is fifty years older then me, he's more like me than a *normal* person of my age could ever be. He's more like me than my parents could ever be.

'My name is Miriam,' I say softly.

'Miriam, nice to meet you. I'm called Georg. And now I'm going up to the organ. So maybe you'll want to scoot.' He stands up and goes to the stairs. 'But I'd be delighted if you'd like to listen.'

Although I don't much like organ music, I stay sitting and listen. It begins softly and slowly. Single long notes which fill the whole building with life. I lean back, relax ...

I had my first piano lesson at seven. At first, I'm terribly proud to be allowed to play the piano. As I get older, I suddenly find it stupid.

It's Joanne who realises. She likes listening to me. Every time she came, I used to play her something. Not now. My piano stands there, untouched.

'Why don't you play any more?' she asks.

At first, I'm a bit shy of telling the truth. Then I confess that I'm ashamed.

'Why?'

I explain that the piano is such a dreadfully classical instrument and that I find it embarrassing to play it.

My answer makes Joanne laugh out loud. I give her a sour look. 'I don't find that one bit funny.'

Then Joanne says something that I will never forget for the rest of my life. 'Miriam, an instrument is not something you can put in a box. It's like everything in your life. It's what you make of it. Of course it's classical. But only if you play classical music on it.'

You have power over your own life. Your life is only as boring or as monotonous as you make it. It's up to you to make something of it.

When I come into the hall at home, I stand still and give a surprised sniff. I slip quickly out of my shoes and jacket and leave them lying where they fall. Then I follow the smell into the living room, where my mother is sitting smiling at me from the couch.

'I'm glad you're back. The delivery came five minutes ago.' She proudly holds up an enormous flat box.

'Pizza special. With ham and mushrooms. And mozzarella. A proper pizza has to have mozzarella.'

Is today some kind of special day? Is it my birthday, maybe? And since when have Mum and I had cosy pizza evenings? Have I missed something?

'Don't look at me like that. Your father is working overtime, and I thought we'd have a girls' night in.'

I raise my eyebrows comically and flop onto the couch beside my mother. 'Do you think this is going to bother him one little bit?'

Why am I saying that, as if this was the most normal situation? The most normal in the world. But at least it feels as if it might get to be normal again. As if it could be completely normal for me to spend evenings like this with my mother.

'There's a woman behind it, wouldn't you think?'

As I nod, she shouts, 'Hah! I knew it! Not even Tomas can be such a workaholic. Do you know her?'

I shake my head. 'Not officially. She was here once or twice, working with him on something. She's actually very nice. Maybe a bit uptight. Oh, and also totally married. I saw her wedding ring.'

At first, I couldn't believe it myself. My father, carrying on with a married woman. My father, of all people. But it makes him happy. So maybe it's OK.

'No! Your father is having an affair with a married woman! I wouldn't have thought he had it in him. Respect.'

I find Mum's reaction totally funny. She's reacting exactly the way I did at the time.

'So, what'll we do this evening?' I ask good-humouredly.

Mum jumps up and yanks a few DVD covers out of her bag. 'I borrowed *Pretty Woman*, *In her Shoes*, *Letters to Julia* and *27 Dresses*.

Ooh, tough choice. 'Can we watch them all?' I bat my eyelashes innocently. It surprises me how easy I'm finding it to talk like this with my mother.

'I wouldn't have got them all otherwise.' Mum is already kneeling in front of the television and is putting in the first DVD. 'But first I'll get us something to drink.'

'Cola or beer?' I shout. My mother swings around, annoyed and disgusted with me. 'Are you mad, girl? You can't drink beer with a good Italian pizza.'

'Vodka?' I ask meekly.

My mother shakes her head, grinning. 'Does Tomas know how well you know your way around the drinks cabinet?

'Please! He thinks I'm still his sweet little girl. He probably thinks I'm still a virgin.'

That thought makes me smile. I spent so many nights at Toby's. And he here with me. But Dad never really twigged. Maybe it was better that way.

'I think I'll have to have a little word with your clueless father,' says Mum, coming back into the living room with a bottle of wine and two glasses. She pours us each a generous glass, and we clink. Then she presses *Play*.

My mother is right. This pizza is unbelievably good.

I only half follow the film. It's far too enjoyable to chat to my mother. I tell her about Dad's affair, about how I fared after the move and how I got to know Toby. And Mum tells me about all the countries she's seen, and I wish the evening would never come to an end. It's really impressive, how many places she's been to.

We didn't manage all four films. I fall asleep during the third one and I only come to when my alarm clock jerks me awake. My father carried me to bed. I have a headache after the two bottles of wine that Mum and I drank.

CHAPTER 16

Today is Tuesday the eighteenth of February. It's thirty-three days since my life changed. That's not so long. One month, in which so much has happened. Really so much. After the shooting, I knew that that experience would change my life. But it was not so much the shooting itself as the decisions that I and people around me have made.

The catalyst for it all, of course, was Mathias Staudt. The fact that we bullied him. Our behaviour has inevitable consequences. Often our deeds are more significant than we think.

I've seen what can happen. What violence can do. And I don't just mean the shooting. I also mean the time before it happened. When I had a perfect life. Back then, when we bullied Mathias Staudt, we destroyed him. I could see, we could all see, what we'd done to him. But I just looked the other way. We never thought how he was feeling. We are to blame for what happened. It is our responsibility.

It's not easy to live with that. To know what we did wrong. And to see it. To realise what others have to live through because of our stupidity. The dead fifth-grade kids. Toby. Their deaths were not without reason. The reason was ourselves. But their deaths were pointless. Toby dug his own grave.

Before we go to school, we're just happy children. We're just the way we are. But as soon as we go to school, that's all over. Then we start to relate to others. We put on particular clothes so that others will like us. Say certain things, because we know that others want to hear them.

School turns us into the people that we will become. We go to particular parties in order to please others. We buy stuff in particular shops. And we ridicule other students, just to belong. Someone always sets the tone. The bitches and the jocks. And they look for one or two victims to diss. And because none of the rest of us want to be one of the victims, we go along with it. We bow to peer pressure.

I can't even say who started it all with Mathias Staudt. He was already an outsider when he started at school. The girls who'd been to primary school with him told us he was disgusting. So we kept him at a distance from the very beginning. We couldn't even be sure it was true, because we didn't get to know him. We just believed it.

I can imagine how it happened. Mathias had some sort of row with the cool guys in first grade. These lads spread rumours about him, and everyone believed them. And it continued like that when he started at high school. Nobody wanted to have anything to do with him.

Mathias was always treated as if he were a piece of dirt. Just because some boy in first grade didn't like him.

I never really thought about it properly, how it came about that Mathias was treated like that. Because I had no interest in Mathias Staudt, as long as I was all right. And that is sad.

Everyone always says it's good to help other people. They talk about moral courage. We're told that everyone is equal. We should treat other people as we would like to be treated ourselves. Then we go to school, and it's 'Keep away from him.' Or 'This would be a better person to make friends with.'

And then at some stage bullying gets discussed in class. Everyone sits there and talks about how appalling they find it, and all the time they are looking right at the boy or girl that they're doing it to. And in the same breath, the teacher puts down some pupil that they can't stand the sight of.

And then when you change schools, they say, 'Don't go to the comprehensive. They're all criminals and foreigners there.'

We keep hearing that all people are equal. But at the same time we're getting the message that we are a bit better. That's sad. It makes me sad. This world is so dishonest. The strong put down the weak. The rich exploit the poor. The powerful use the powerless. It will never change. It's a vicious circle. And nobody can get out of it.

We bullied Mathias Staudt for lots of different reasons. Some of us so that they wouldn't feel so insignificant themselves. Others because they were afraid they would be dissed themselves if they didn't go along with it. And others again did it because they enjoyed having power over weaker people. I never really thought it through. I never really thought about how he must have been feeling. I just did it, and I don't even know why. Maybe because everyone was doing it. For me it was harmless. But look what it has led to. My current life. So my thoughtless behaviour has destroyed my life.

We are going through hell, day by day. My dad can't understand that. And as for my mum – I'm not really ready to trust her fully yet. Nobody in our families can ever understand us. We can never lean on their shoulder and bawl our eyes out. I don't even want to. I don't want to cry about it. I want to think as little as possible about it. To get back to normal.

I want to live again. To feel again.

I want to feel Toby again. His kisses. His hugs. To see his smile. To hear his laugh, his funny comments. I want to feel his hand in mine. I want to relive the moment in which I first saw him, on holiday. And the moment that I fell in love with him. Our first date. And our first kiss. His mouth, when he says *I love you*. And his eyes, when he looks at me as if I am the best thing that has ever happened to him.

I'd like to just turn the clock back. And relive last year

over and over again, on a loop. Because it was the best year of my life. And I want my life back.

I'd like to be able to see the world the way I used to. Because, stupid as it sounds, the world seems totally different. More garish. More superficial. Bigger.

The world sounds totally different now. Louder. More dangerous. Sadder.

The world feels totally different now. Colder. More hopeless. Rawer.

I want my life back. And time.

I think I understand now how Mathias Staudt felt for all those years.

School is tough today. Joanne is missing for the third day in a row. And in the second period my English teacher shouts at me for a good five minutes in front of everyone, all because I've forgotten my homework. In the third period, we have to listen to a lecture on solidarity. And in the fourth, one of our classmates collapses and has to be fetched home by her mother.

I'm really ready for the holidays. Or at least for a very, very strong cup of coffee. Instead of that, Sophia calls me to join her between the containers after school. Of course that would have to happen today.

I turn around crossly to her and bark, 'What do you want?'

I am disgusted by her. What has happened to this girl

who used to be my friend? She has bloodshot eyes, lank hair, pale, mottled skin. I can't understand why she is doing this to herself. Why she hates herself so much. The girl I know has simply vanished.

I don't want to look at her. It grieves me to have to see, day in, day out, how the people who are closest to my heart are letting themselves go. I don't want to see either Sophia or Joanne. But then if they're missing, as Joanne has been for the last few days, I worry about them.

'I only want to talk.' Sophia raises her hands, as if to fend off blame. 'But you just ignore me the whole time, never come near me during break, just shout at me when I want to talk to you.'

There's a lot I could say back to her. For example, that she's in a weird mood (which definitely has to do with all the grass she smokes). Or that she doesn't come near me at break either. Or that I can't imagine what we could have to talk about, as we have nothing in common any more.

In one second, so many things occur to me that I could accuse her of. But I don't do it. I don't want any discussion with her. So I just shrug my shoulders.

But Sophia doesn't give up. She always loved playing power games. She was always good at showing others that they are worth less than she is. Only I've never been one of her victims.

'But I miss you so much.' Even a deaf person could hear the sarcasm in her voice. 'Why don't we do something together again?'

I give her the finger and am about to go when the façade suddenly drops and I see the Sophia I know. She looks at me. With her big, sad eyes. A tear runs down her face.

'Don't think badly of me,' she whispers. 'It hurts so much, Miriam.'

She's going to say more, only that Vanessa suddenly appears. She gives me a weird look. Sophia's face gets hard again and she starts acting confident.

'So, Miriam, darling. You know where to find me. It would be a shame if we didn't do stuff together any more.'

Then she sails away like a queen.

'What's all that about, if you don't mind?' asks Vanessa.

'I think the real Sophia is still in there. And she's in a terrible way,' I say, looking after Sophia.

'What was that?'

I'm laughing so much that I have to hang onto Sophia in order to catch my breath. Tanja's mouth is open in shock. The guy that Sophia has been chatting up is extremely hot.

'Oh my God, Sophia, please tell me that you are going to phone that guy.' Tanja is so excited, she's shaking Sophia.

But Sophia just shrugs and throws the guy's phone number in the nearest bin. So that Tanja can't have it.

'Please tell me that you didn't really do that!' Tanja's voice is bursting with hilarity. She split up with her boyfriend a month previously and she is sleeping with anyone and everyone, out of sheer exasperation. She certainly wouldn't have let a guy like that go.

'I wouldn't have rung him anyway.' Sophia shrugs her shoulders.

I can't stop laughing. Tanja's expression is priceless. We're on our way to Pimkie. Our flip-flops are flapping. We're all wearing big sunglasses. And we each have at least three shopping bags. I love the summer.

'Have you still got that number?' Tanja starts again.

'Oh, please! If he wants something from me, he can think up something a bit more original. I can get something better if I want to. Boys only ever want the one thing from me. So they should at least have to work to get it.'

Sophia doesn't let just any old boy near her, unlike Tanja, who has more guys than I can count. And every time she thinks, *This time it's The One*. But it never lasts longer than a month.

'Oh, really?' Tanja raises her eyebrows in amusement. 'Do you think so? Prove it. How about that guy there.' She nods towards a boy who is leaning against a wall with two of his mates and a girl. The boy is extremely good-looking. Dark blond hair. A good six foot, muscular, tanned. The kind of guy you wouldn't have the nerve to approach because he would definitely have a girlfriend already.

There's a wicked glint in Sophia's eye. She loves a challenge. Especially if she has a good chance. Which she has, because she can always manage to twist guys around her little finger when she wants to.

'What am I supposed to do?'

'Get me his number.'

'OK.' Sophia walks slowly backwards, looking Tanja in the eye all the time. 'Nothing could be easier.'

She turns around and goes over to him. Tanja and I watch her, mesmerised.

'You know she'll do it, no problem.' That's not a question, it's a statement. Of course Tanja knows it.

'Yes, I know. But I love watching her. Guys always go to pieces.'

Sophia starts to chat to the guy. A bit of twiddling here and there. A coquettish laugh. A flick of an eyelash. The guy is like putty in Sophia's hands.

It only takes five minutes till Sophia comes back. With the number. Tanja and I can't stop laughing. Then Tanja disappears briefly, because she has to go to the loo, she's laughed so much.

'I'll tell you a secret, but you mustn't tell Tanja,' says Sophia, as Tanja disappears from view.

I nod and look curiously at Sophia.

'I flirted with him a bit at first and then I asked him for his number. But I told the guy the truth. That I had a bet on with my friend. That's the only reason he gave me his number.'

I look at Sophia sideways. Does she really believe that? Then she's really blind and hasn't noticed how the guy looked at her. But it's like her, to have told the boy the truth. Sophia is always direct and doesn't beat about the bush. And that's the thing I love about her most.

Sophia really got together with that guy. They were still together when the shooting happened. I don't know how things are between them now.

CHAPTER 17

Grandma and Grandpa come on a visit. I haven't seen them for a while and hug them hard. It does me good to see their faces. Grandpa's face is so wise and Grandma's so understanding.

It's really not all that very long since I used to think that these two could protect me from anything. But everyone wakes up one day to the realisation that they are alone and defenceless.

We sit in the kitchen. Mum makes tea. Dad is working. That's nothing new. It feels almost like the way things used to be. To sit at the table, drink tea, chat – that helps me, it's worth a hundred consultations with Dr Frei.

There's a sudden ring at the doorbell. Mum gets up and opens the door. I don't know who I was expecting it to be, but I certainly never thought it would be Joanne's father. He comes into the kitchen behind my mother. He looks tired, exhausted. Bags under his eyes, stringy grey hair, eyes cloudy. He seems smaller than he really is.

My mum asks him to sit down. He sinks onto a chair and looks me in the eye. I know what's coming. This is not the first time I've experienced this. People look like this only in very particular situations. On that day, on that one terrible day, I saw this expression in the faces of police officers, doctors, officials.

'Miriam.'

I can tell what he is going to say. But at the same time, I can't take it in. To get certainty, and to prevent him having to utter the hard words, I ask, 'Is she dead?'

He nods. 'Yes.'

There's no more to be said. I know I will weep later, but not now. Now I have to try to understand.

The pain doesn't come immediately, or at least not all of the pain. Nowhere near the whole pain. Only when I'm alone in my room will the pain come. Then I'll think about Joanne. Think of all the things we have lived through together. And I will cry about the girl who was my best friend.

'What happened?'

Actually, it's not important. It doesn't matter, it won't change anything. Still, I'd like to know.

'She slashed her wrists.'

'Oh, God!' My grandma claps her hands over her mouth in horror. She gives Grandpa a despairing look. He prises away her clenched hand and holds it in his. Then he reaches for my hand too and strokes it soothingly.

Mum stands up and starts cleaning the kitchen counter. What do you say? What do you say when anything you say only makes it worse. 'I'm so sorry.' I have no more words. Joanne has taken her life.

'That's just nuts.'

Amused, I turn to Joanne, who is sitting next to me. Sophia, Tanja and Vanessa are sitting in front of us. All three of them have tears in their eyes.

I'm close to tears myself. I'm surprised that Joanne, of all people, is unmoved by the scene that is playing on the stage. Normally, she's the first to burst into tears. In the Easter holidays, we watched *Titanic* together. Joanne started crying at the point where the ship hits the iceberg. And she didn't stop until an hour after the film was over.

'It's totally romantic.' I contradict her softly.

'Sure, it's so romantic when he kills himself because he thinks she is dead, and then she kills herself because he is really dead. I didn't kill myself when my boyfriend left me,' she whispers back.

Surely she's not comparing herself to Romeo and Juliet!

'They do it because they can't live without each other.'

'That's so cowardly. To kill yourself is absolutely cowardly. People are just running away from their lives.'

Now it's Joanne who has run away from her life.

I look out of the window. The snow is melted. A spider is spinning a web outside on the window frame. I watch it closely. I don't much like spiders. I usually scream when I find a spider in the house. Joanne always used to carry them out for me. She'd hold them very carefully.

Joanne is dead. To take it in, I keep saying it over and over in my head. *Joanne is dead. Dead is Joanne. Is Joanne dead? Joanne dead is. D-e-a-d. J-o-a-n-n-e. I-s.* Depending on the order in which you say these words, you get different utterances. Some of them make no sense. Some do.

Joanne and I used to mix up the words in sentences. It was a game we played. The funniest things used to emerge. But you can twist and turn these words all you like: they stay serious and sad.

'We've already buried Joanne. Just the two of us. Dana wanted us to be alone with her.'

Joanne's father's voice brings me back to our kitchen. I look out of the window again. The spider is moving swiftly and daintily, as her web gets more beautiful and majestic. Life goes on, even if we don't want it to.

'Miriam, did Joanne give any indication? Should we have known?'

'Only if you are mind-readers,' I answer bitterly. It is hard. But it is the truth. 'I mean, she never opened her mouth after the shooting. We'll never know what was going on in her head.'

Harald is rooting in his pockets. Then he pulls something out. White and pretty crumpled.

'She left goodbye letters. One for us and one for you.'

He holds it out to me. I recognise Joanne's writing on

the white envelope: *Miriam*. I am incapable of moving. When I don't take it, Harald lays the letter on the table with a sigh. 'You were her best friend. I am glad Joanne had you.'

I just nod, reach for the letter. My arms feel incredibly heavy and stiff. My hands are shaking. I'm not sure if I want to know what's in it. I run up to my room, because I can't stand it any longer with my family and Harald.

I bang the door and sink to the floor. I'm breathing fast. Tears are brimming in my eyes. Suddenly I feel really sick. I take a few deep breaths in and out. Then I tear the envelope open.

My dearest best friend

Do you remember that summer three years ago? We got ourselves a giant map of the world and hung it downstairs in the basement of your house. In our room, where nobody except us ever went. We marked all the cities and countries that we wanted to visit. And we stuck on photos of monuments and places that we wanted to see. We played that we were already there.

For me, it's going to be a game for ever. I'll never see any of those places. But you will. You will travel around the world for both of us.

I am so unbelievably sorry. About everything that happened on *that* day and before. I just can't live with the guilt. Believe me, I've tried. Please don't be angry that I'm going. I just can't go on. Perhaps it's cowardly of me just to vanish. I think I understand Romeo and Juliet better now. They killed themselves because there was nothing beautiful left in their lives. And with me it's just the same. I couldn't ever live properly again. I'll say hello to Toby for you, up there where things go on after death.

Live for us both. Love for us both. Do all the things you want to do. And don't let anything stop you. You can do anything. You always could.

Joanne

I rock myself back and forth. An almost animal noise comes from my throat. And then the tears start to flow.

I think about that summer three years back, when Joanne and I hung the map in my basement, in our room, which we stuffed with pillows and blankets. We played at travelling the world, seeing all the magic places.

I think of Joanne's laughter and of how we used to lie on my bed and talk about boys and clothes, when we'd got too old to play in the basement.

I think about the time Joanne gave Toby a piece of her mind in break-time, when I was having a fight with him. And how she always used to be there for me. How I knew her better than anyone else. How it was exactly the same the other way around.

And I think about how Joanne couldn't live any longer with the guilt. The guilt that also burdens me. Even though Joanne was one of those who never really treated Mathias badly. Unlike me. And Toby.

Nothing lasts in life. Not even my best friend. Absolutely nothing.

I sit on the floor, sobbing, holding the letter, which has got all wet with my tears. I'm holding my stomach, because it hurts so much. As much as it did a month ago, when Toby died. Now I've lost them both. They're gone. For ever.

Joanne was afraid that I might be angry with her. I understand exactly what she means. I almost envy her that she has had the courage to end it all.

I'd like it all to be over for me too. I don't want to go on losing everything. But to die – I don't want that either. I want to turn back the clock. Back to the summer, when everything was OK. Everything wonderful, perfect.

I'm tired. So tired. My heart is raw. Raw and in despair. I curl up on the floor, clutching the letter to my chest, and close my eyes.

Then I suddenly hear this melody in my head. It is a melancholy piece by a French composer. Joanne used to love it. She made me play it for her for hours on end.

I get up slowly and sit at the piano. I open the lid and stroke the keys. Then I start to play.

It takes a while for my fingers to get used to the movements. They've lost their flexibility. But they soon regain their confidence, the way they used to be, and they seem to find the right notes all by themselves. My whole being seems to appreciate the sorrowful melody. As if I am playing it just for Joanne.

I finish the piece and only then do I notice that Mum is standing in the doorway, listening. I've no idea how long she's been listening for.

'I didn't know you still played,' she says, sitting beside me on the piano stool.

'I haven't been,' I answer, touching the keys wistfully. 'Not till now.'

Why? A simple word. Three letters. No more. But what if this word won't get out of your head? When it's there, everywhere, all the time, it can have a lot of power over you. It can swallow you up.

I had just started to let this word go. To accept life the way it is. But now it seems to me as if life has it in for me. As if a higher power wants to make me do penance for some sin. But I don't believe in that sort of shit.

Joanne is dead. Just gone. Like Toby. Everyone I love simply disappears. Disappears for ever. Toby and Joanne. Now I have two graves to visit.

I'd better be careful not to turn into a ghost myself, I spend so much time in the cemetery. Often enough to know that the widow of the grave next to Toby's comes every second day at exactly three o'clock and stays half an hour. Sometimes she brings her grandchildren. Twins. I guess they're three or four years old.

The pastor does his rounds here every Friday at about four o'clock in the afternoon, and at least every second week there's a burial.

This morning, I was at Joanne's grave. A white gravestone, with gold-engraved lettering:

All growing is a dying,
All becoming is a passing,
Every leaving a return,
Every death a resurrection.

I have thought a lot about the meaning of life. I've wondered why I live. Why we all live. Whether it's just chance whom we love and what we do. Whether it's just a coincidence that we bullied Mathias Staudt and that he shot at us. Naturally I haven't arrived at an answer. I'd really like to do what Joanne asked me to do. I'd like to live for us both. But I don't know how. I miss her so much.

This afternoon, I tell all this to Dr Frei. She looks dismayed. But she listens to me, without interrupting. Every now and then she gives an understanding nod.

When I finally stop talking, she asks, 'Do you feel you have to achieve that? Do you feel as if Joanne has put pressure on you?'

I think about that. 'In a way. Some people are saying how well I am coping with the situation. But I don't feel that's true. When they say that, I feel everyone just expects me to keep on going.'

'For them maybe it *is* just to be expected. For everyone else, after all, life is just going on, as normal. At the moment, such terrible things have happened and you and I are just talking, and at the same time, lots of wonderful things are also happening. Before that shooting happened at your school, life wasn't perfect. There were problems. You had to get through puberty without a mother. Your father never had much time for you. But that was all right with you, because there were good things too. School. Your boyfriend. Your friends. These things no longer apply. A person you knew tried to shoot you. Your whole sense of trust in the world has been shaken by this. And now you have to rebuild this trust. That's a process that will take years.

'You've started to accept it, which is very good. That's a big step. You can be really proud of yourself. Now you have to find lovely things in life. That won't make the things that have happened any less dreadful – I don't want to seem to give you false hope. But this burden will seem lighter if you can find people with whom you can share it. And gradually you will get your confidence back.'

She's right. Even before the shooting, bad things did happen. But in spite of that, my life was fine, because there was also a lot of good stuff in it.

'What would you like to do, Miriam?'

This question comes out of the blue and it floors me. I'm not sure what she means. 'Now?'

'Yes. Or tomorrow. Or next week. What do you really love?'

'Holidays,' I say, without thinking. But that is right. I want a break from school.

Dr Frei nods. 'And why is that?'

'I need peace. A bit of distance.' I think for a moment. 'It would be good to get away.'

Dr Frei just smiles. The way she always smiles. 'Well then, do it. That should appeal to your parents too.'

I look at her doubtfully. 'Will it change anything?'

'Just give it a try.'

CHAPTER 18

I'm really here. I'm at the place that I came to almost every day for the past five years. The place where I have had thousands of successes and failures. Fights with my friends. Trouble with Toby. Conflicts with teachers. But also lots of things that Joanne and I helped with. Shows, collections for charity. There was always something to be organised. Good grades. Class outings. Over the past five years, a large part of my life took place here.

I feel as if I can't breathe. That's all because I'm at school, at the scene of the crime. The closer I got to this place, the worse it got. And now I'm here, at this dreadful place. I'd want to go in. But at the same time I don't want to. I want both to go in and not to go in. I don't know what I want.

It looks so different from how it looked a month ago. In the meantime, it's become a building site. At first sight you'd hardly recognise the school. It looks like an enormous sandpit.

I know that the city council is having it all completely renovated, in order to annihilate the traumatic memories.

But I don't think that's possible. The very thought that this is where the shooting happened is enough to give me a sinking feeling in my stomach. Whether or not the school looks different really doesn't matter. It makes no difference.

I'm not supposed to be here. There's a security fence and in front of it a sign says 'Building site. No entry.' But the builders left off work ages ago.

I stand directly in front of the main entrance. There used to be a massive wooden door here, almost like a gate. Now it's gone. So that we won't be reminded of *before*.

I could cross the threshold. But the first step is hard. It's the film in my head that prevents me. I can hear the shouts. And the silence. The wretched silence before Mathias Staudt entered the boys' toilet on the first floor in order to shoot Philip Schwarz. The fear feels real, as real as if the shooting is happening at this very moment. I feel obliged to turn around and make sure that nobody is standing behind me with a gun. A thousand feelings rise up again, rob me of my breath. I realise that I'm about to have a panic attack. My heart starts to race.

But then I take a step forward. I've crossed an invisible boundary. I didn't think I could do it. But I have done it.

I need a moment to make something out in the twilight. It doesn't look as I expected it to. There is no furniture in the corridors. The pictures that the pupils painted have been taken down. It's just a bare, half-finished renovated room.

Everything is different. But the memories remain. When I look at the front door, feelings pull me in that I can't control. When I look along the corridor again, thoughts take hold of me that I cannot shake off.

Well, here I am. I haven't been able to sleep all night. I've been looking forward to this day for two years, the day I change to secondary school. And now the time has come, and it doesn't feel so great after all.

I couldn't sleep all night with excitement. I expected that I would feel different now. Bigger. After all, I'm a secondary student now. But the truth is, I feel small and insignificant. I am one of a hundred and thirty first years, and I have no idea who the others are.

Suppose I don't make any friends. What if they think I'm a freak. Maybe the girls will all be nasty to me and the boys will push me around.

I look around nervously. Lots of my classmates know each other since primary school, but I only moved here in the summer holidays, because my parents separated. Since then, I haven't seen my mum. I wouldn't admit it for anything, but I miss her.

Sometimes when Dad is working and doesn't notice what I'm doing, I pull out the old photo albums from when we were still a family. And imagine what it would be like to feel happy again. A happy family. Since Mum left us, I've only had a birthday card and a Christmas card from her. At first I cried a lot, but I quickly realised that made Dad even sadder, so I stopped.

My dad and I have moved in with my grandparents in my father's home town. It does me good to see my grandma and grandpa every day. It helps a bit anyway.

And now, here I am in my new school. It's September. The start of the school year. My dad thinks I'll make friends easily. I'm not so sure.

My grandmother touches my shoulder. 'Look, see that sign where it says 5A? That's your class. Go on in. We'll stay here.'

I look at her, unsure of myself, but Grandma smiles encouragingly. My knees like jelly, I go in to the entrance hallway. There are children standing around, talking to each other. I stand near them. It's nuts, I know, but I suddenly start to cry.

'Hey,' says a girl, who has been talking to another girl. She turns to me and gives me a hanky. She has dark curls and very pale blue eyes.

'Come on, we're not that bad.'

I smile shyly at her, wiping away my tears.

'I'm Joanne and this is Sophia,' she says.

Now I look at the other girl. She is quite thin and has light blond short hair. Joanne, on the other hand, is rather plump. She has dark skin and a turned-up nose. The two of them are wearing the same T-shirt with a distorted yellow smiley-face on it.

Joanne notices where I am looking. 'Cool, isn't it? We bought these T-shirts together. In the holidays.'

I just nod.

'What's your name? Where did you go to primary school? I've never seen you before.'

They look at me curiously. They really seem to be interested.

'I'm Miriam. I'm not from here. My dad and I just moved here.'

'Are your parents divorced?' Another girl comes up to us. She has wavy brown hair that reaches her waist. Dark green eyes.

Again I just nod.

'Mine too. For the past six months. At the weekend I live with my father and during the week with my mother. I'm Vanessa by the way.'

'But you didn't go to our school, did you?' Joanne asks her.

'No. I live out of town.'

'There's Tanja, my neighbour.' Sophia points to a girl with long red hair who is coming towards us. She's tall. Almost a head taller than me.

Vanessa gives her a delighted wave. Tanja waves back.

'How come you know Tanja?' Sophia sounds surprised.

'We do guitar together.'

'You play the guitar?' asks Joanne, charmed. 'I've always wanted to play percussion, but my mother makes me learn the violin instead. The drums are too noisy for her.'

'I play the piano.' I'm delighted to be able to join in the conversation.

'Really? I have to come around to your place. I want to hear you playing. And to tinkle a bit myself,' cries Joanne.

And Sophia adds, 'I'm coming too.'

I'm not so scared any more. The whole class all seems really nice, although I still don't know many of them. The whole year seems super. For heaven's sake, the whole school!

I turn a full circle and take a good look at everyone. So many pupils who are just getting to know each other. Make friends.

Then I see a boy. Small, fat, with unwashed hair and glasses. He's standing in the furthest corner of the school hall. He looks sad.

'That's Mathias.' Sophia has noticed where I'm looking. 'He's from our school. Better keep out of his way.'

'He's obnoxious,' Joanne adds. 'He used to pick his nose, even in fourth grade. Yuck.' Joanne pretends to hold her nose. 'There's some stink when he lets a fart. And he does that all the time. It doesn't even seem to embarrass him.'

I look at the boy again. I feel sorry for him. But I am new at this school and I need to get into the swing.

'Hey, Miriam. Let's all sit together.'

I smile happily at Vanessa. I belong now.

I never gave any serious thought to how Mathias must have felt. I ... well, I didn't even want to think about it. I didn't want to know what loneliness felt like. Who wants to? We just went along with it. We just did what everyone did.

I turn around slowly, looking closely at everything. The protective covering that is supposed to keep the floor from getting paint on it rustles under my feet. I close my eyes and spin. Faster. And faster. There's only me and the wind that my spinning creates. I spin until I fall. Then I stay sitting.

This is where Joanne and I met. In this enormous hall. This is exactly where I saw Mathias Staudt for the first time. Who would have thought that it would end like this? Who could have had the least idea what a child would ultimately have been capable of?

CHAPTER 19

Easter holidays. Pale green leaves rustle in the trees. The fields are dotted with wildflowers. Insects are humming and buzzing. I've longed for spring for so long. But now that it's here, it's even lovelier than I've remembered. The sun drives away bad thoughts.

We've all started packing like mad. I'm sitting in a muddle of clothes, jewellery and sunglasses. It's bloody early. Half past six. Normally I wouldn't get up so early on a Saturday. But we're planning to leave in two hours. I'm in an incredible mood. I don't know where we're going on holiday but it has to be somewhere in Germany, because we're going by car and we're packing both bathing things and jackets.

I throw things randomly into my suitcase: my green jacket, my black jeans, my blue sunglasses, my white ballerina flats, my pink-spotted top, my denim skirt, leggings, well-worn Vans ...

I still can't quite believe it. I'm really going away. I'm getting out of here. I could dance like mad around the room, singing loudly. I haven't been so happy for a long time. Just for the happy hell of it, I throw my snuggly socks I got from Grandma into my suitcase too.

Then my glance falls on my denim-blue pumps and I shout down the hall, 'Mum, can I wear pumps wherever we're going?'

'Sure! You can always wear pumps. I'm taking two pairs myself.'

I give a start, because Mum's voice is directly behind me. She's standing, smiling, in the doorway. She's wearing a flowered tunic and white jeans. And strappy sandals with almost no heel. She's put her hair up.

I make a spirited attempt to close my suitcase. But the zip won't close.

'Damn!' I press down on the mountain of clothes and try again.

'Try sitting on it.'

'Thank you. I'm that fat, am I?' I ask in disgust and sit on the case. It must look funny. I crane my neck and yank at the zip. It doesn't budge.

'Could you please help me. Instead of standing there grinning like Lady Muck?'

'Pull up your legs and make yourself heavy.' Mum is kneeling in front of my case. 'Oh, God, Miriam, the suitcase is just too small. Have you not got a bigger one?'

I look aghast at my extra large case. 'I don't think there *is* a bigger size.'

We change our tactics and sit together on the case.

'What are you doing?' Dad is standing in the doorway,

looking disbelievingly at us. 'You know we're only going for a week.

'You're travelling with two women. What do you expect?'

Just at that moment, the zip moves.

'Yes!'

'At last,' cries Mum, relieved.

'So could we have breakfast now?' asks Dad.

Two hours later, we're on the motorway on our way to our destination. Wherever that may be. I sit on the back seat and look out of the window. My parents are sitting in front, squabbling like children about music.

The countryside speeds by. Hills, fields, villages and woods. I lean my head against the window and breathe out with relief. It is a liberating feeling to leave home further and further behind me. I close my eyes and can see only dark and light stripes. Sun and shade. Sun and shade.

I don't wake up until my father drives off the motorway. I have really slept the whole time and have no idea how long we've been travelling.

I look around curiously. We're definitely still in Germany. There's a placard that says 'Farm-fresh eggs' in German on it. There are lots of fields. Crooked trees are swaying in the wind.

It looks so different from the area where I live. The

sight of the strange landscape sets something free inside me. It's an incredible feeling to be so far away from home. How far doesn't matter. Just away. I smile.

Maybe this is exactly what I need. A few days to myself. Just me. And my parents. No school. No area that I know like the back of my hand.

Something wonderful and blue suddenly appears before my eyes. And birds. Birds circling over the blue. And mudflats. Shoreline.

'The sea!' I yell, delighted. I just can't help myself. We're at the Baltic. This is where we've been going.

The sea. For me, there's nothing lovelier. The wind, the roar of the sea, the screeching of gulls, the sunsets. Even the rain is better at the sea than it is at home. Oh, I love the sea. The sea has always been a magic place for me. I feel free here.

We drive on for half an hour through villages and countryside. Then we stop in Büsum. I yank the car door open and run out, yelling. Normally, I would be embarrassed to do that, but now I can't help myself. I hop around in circles. I shout out to my parents, 'I love you! You are fabulous. I love, love, LOVE you! I love the sea. I just LOVE the whole WORLD.'

I have no idea why I'm yelling like this. I just have to let it out.

I yank my suitcase and a handbag out of the car boot and stumble with the luggage towards the house that Dad is just opening up. It is a little red-brick house. There's a nice front garden with daffodils and multi-coloured tulips. It has a thatched roof.

I get a green shock when I go inside. Everything is green. Green walls, green pictures, green cushions. Only the furniture is white. There are flowers everywhere. I turn around and look at it all. The living room. The little kitchen. The narrow bedroom. And the bathroom. I couldn't live here permanently. All the green would drive me mad. But for a week, it's perfect. It really goes with the spring.

A narrow, creaky wooden staircase leads to a room with crossbeams, also painted all in green. In the middle of the green room is a double bed. Against the walls are a wardrobe, a dressing table, an armchair and a coat-stand. There's another door, behind which is concealed a second bathroom.

Mum, Dad and I quickly agree that we women will take the attic room. Then we unpack. Mum puts on a radio, which is on her bedside table. The Beatles' 'Lucy in the Sky with Diamonds' is just playing. We turn the radio up a bit, because we both love that song, and, dancing, we put our things into the wardrobe. We have a minor disagreement about how to divide up the space. But it's not serious. We're only teasing each other.

'Oh my God!' I grab hold of the thong that my mother is taking out of her bag. Leopard-skin print. In front anyway. Behind there's pretty well nothing.

'You can't seriously be going to wear that?'

'Why not? Men like that kind of thing.' Mum shrugs her shoulders.

'But the straps must be totally uncomfortable.'

'So what? And these, by the way, are not all that different.' She holds up a pair of my pants. They are more lace than anything else. She's right. They are also hot. And I only bought them because of Toby. But still, not in the same category as my mother's thong.

Does your father know you own things like this? You're only fifteen. He should take better care of you.'

'And does he know about you?' I ask cheekily, taking the pants from her and stick them into the cupboard.

In the evening, we go to a little restaurant. We order fish, sitting outdoors, not thirty metres from the harbour. Happily, I watch the boats sailing on the water. How lovely it all is! The smell of the fishing boats isn't even annoying. It belongs here. Without it, something would be missing.

The ocean glitters in the sinking sun. The sky is turning a light orange. Gulls are screeching overhead. The wind is blowing over the town. And the sea is roaring. It's always like this at the seaside.

As always.

CHAPTER 20

'Hey, sleepyhead, wake up!'

I mutter and turn onto my other side. I don't want to get up yet. I haven't slept so well for ages. Dreamless.

'Come on. You don't want to sleep your holidays away.'

I open my eyes. Oh, yes, holidays. We're at the sea. The sun is shining on my face. I can hear the birds singing through the window and, if you listen hard, the screeching of the seagulls down at the sea.

I give a satisfied sigh and turn over. Mum is sitting on the other side of the bed, her hair all tousled. I have to laugh at how she looks.

'Don't laugh. You don't look much better. It's no secret how women look in the mornings, without makeup.'

I raise my hands. 'I didn't say a word.'

I go into the bathroom and turn on the shower.

'And who said you could shower first?'

I stick my head out and say, 'I did.'

And I duck back into the shower to avoid the sock that my mother has thrown at me. I can hear her coming into the bathroom and turning on the tap to wash her teeth.

She throws me a towel when I get out of the shower. I wrap myself in the fluffy towelling and take another towel to dry my hair with. Through the window the sun is shining brightly into my face, making me squinch my eyes. The sun's rays feel very warm on my skin through the glass. Almost too warm, like summer sunshine.

Mum is under the shower. The sweet floral scent of her shower gel fills the whole room and the window is fogging up.

I wipe the steam from the mirror with the flat of my hand. It's been a long time since I've looked at my reflection without wanting to run away from it. The rings around my eyes don't seem so dark. My eyes are livelier.

I start to poke around in my makeup bag for a stick of concealer. But then I change my mind, so I just give my eyelashes a light brush of mascara and leave the rest as it is.

There's a bit of a tussle between Mum and me because one mirror in a bathroom is obviously one too few. I do something that I've never done before with my new hairstyle: two plaits. My hair has grown just long enough to take the teeny pigtails. The bits at the front that are too short spring back out. I don't care.

I think today, I'm not going to care about a thing. Not from the usual lack of interest that sometimes gets hold of me, but because I'm happy in my skin. I feel good just the way I am.

Mum and I lay the table for breakfast outside on

the patio. The day is far too lovely to begin it indoors. Dad jokes that we look like we are going to a fashion show, we're looking so chic. He only pipes down and makes the coffee when Mum gives him a smack with a breadboard.

I'm never going on holiday with you two again!' cries Dad. I shake my head, laughing. We're in a shopping area. The buildings are all three or four storeys high, so that the sun can't penetrate properly. It's really cold in the shade, and I get goose pimples.

It's a pleasant, quiet day. Not so many tourists turn up at the Baltic in the Easter holidays. Either they go to Switzerland for the snow or they're tanning themselves on a beach in Hawaii.

My hands are weighed down with ten thousand shopping bags, bursting with souvenirs, jewellery, clothes and food. I'm cooking this evening.

'Your father is going to start exaggerating!' Mum rolls her eyes.

'Exaggerate?' Dad looks at her disbelievingly. 'You said you'd get something for dinner. And you've bought nothing but junk that will only gather dust at home.'

I bite my lip to stop myself laughing again. What did Dad expect? He went to town with two women.

'It's nice junk.' I give him my darling-daughter smile.

He shrugs. 'You've spent a small fortune.'

'If you have a problem with that, maybe you shouldn't let us anywhere near the shops.'

As if he could stop us!

And then, at last, I'm at the sea. The wind is blowing my hair into my face. The sea is roaring. A feeling of unbelievable calm comes over me when I hear the steady roar of the waves. I gather shells of every shape and colour. I haven't felt so full of life for ages.

'Get a load of those two!' calls my mother. 'They are a sandwich short of a picnic.' She's looking at a pair of mad people, who are actually going swimming at 12 degrees Celsius.

I just take off my shoes and run into the water. I don't care that I'm going to get sopping wet. My jeans are soaking up the water and get very heavy. It's really cold. At first I wince because it's like being pricked by a thousand needles. But I get used to the temperature very quickly.

Mum stands there, her mouth open. Then she laughs and follows me. We splash each other. We're screeching like two little girls. We *feel* like two little girls.

'For heaven's sake, get out of the water! It's way too cold.'

Dad is right, it is far too cold. But I don't give a damn.

'You're so wet, you can walk home. I'm not letting you into the car.'

Mum looks at me, her eyebrows raised, her eyes shining. Even though the water is cold, I'm filled with warmth. Because life is so lovely. Lovely and terrible at the same time.

'Come on, Dad! Don't be such a spoilsport. Come in!'

'You can't have it all. Someone will have to look after you when you get pneumonia.'

At that we grab my father and drag him headfirst into the sea. We're laughing loudly, triumphantly. My father stands up, spitting out sand and water. But he's laughing too. Then he grabs me and ducks my head under water. And Mum – the traitor! – helps him! The three of us have never laughed so much together. Never.

In the evening, we sit on the terrace and play a game. Everyone has a slip of paper stuck to their forehead with the name of a personality on it. You have to guess who you are. Dad hasn't really got the idea. He is Lady Gaga. That's not fair for his first time. And Mum is Simba from *The Lion King*. She will guess that one easily. A long time ago, she had to watch that film over and over again with me because I loved it so much.

Mum sticks my name onto my forehead. She thought it up. Frowning, Dad looks at us both and shakes his head with a smile.

'What?' I ask.

'Nothing.' He looks happy. 'You're first.'

I start to guess. 'Am I an animal?'

Dad nods. 'Yes.'

Mum chose my name ... and on her bedside table is one of the *Twilight* books. 'Am I Jacob Black?'

My mother laughs. 'No, you're not a werewolf. My turn. Am I human?'

'No.'

'What about me?'

'Yes, Dad.'

My mother lays a hand on my shoulder. 'Well, I wouldn't be so sure about that.'

I laugh out loud. You can't be sure about Lady Gaga.

It's my turn again. 'Am I a woman?'

'Yes.'

'Definitely. Am I an animal?'

'Yes.'

'Am I a man?'

'No.'

'Hm, well, it's not easy to say exactly.'

'Am I a TV star?'

'Am I female?'

Am I, am I, am I ... The questions keep coming. After ten minutes, I know I'm a character from a TV programme. Maybe from *Twilight*? I can't guess it. There are so many film characters. In any case, my parents are laughing their heads off and keep saying it's totally easy.

'Oh, Mum, I just can't get it.'

'Do you give up?'

'Yes.'

'Nala.'

'Nala?' What? I look at Mum, astonished.

'Yes. You know, the lioness from *The Lion King*. Have you forgotten how often we watched it? Mum has had the same idea as me. She's remembered the same beautiful moment as I did. I can't help it. I start to laugh. And also to cry a little.

'Oh, Mum!' I cry and fall on her neck. Now we're both crying. I'd *never* have thought it. Maybe she wasn't such a bad mother. And now she's back.

The loser has to do the wash-up. As I'm washing the dishes, I look at the view out of the kitchen window. A cat runs across the road. A car drives by. Gulls circle in the sky. My parents are chatting. Life goes on. Onwards, always onwards. Sometimes life seems to be over. but it's not so. Life keeps on going. And at some stage, when we feel better, we join in again. There is only one rule that we have to know. Life doesn't wait. For anyone.

It's not in our hands how long we live. Death just comes one day. For some people it's a surprise. For others it comes slowly. For some it's swift and painless. For others full of suffering and fear. We don't know *when* or *how* we will die. All we can decide is what to do with the time we are given.

After the washing up I go out again, barefoot. I have only one thing with me. A bottle with the letter in it.

I walk along the road, over a sandy filed, up a slope to the dunes. Then I run along the beach.

Dusk has been falling for ages. It will soon be dark. The wind is stronger than this morning. The sea is restless, agitated.

As I walk along the beach, I step on shells and stones. Once I stand on something pointy. It hurts, but I don't take any notice.

My breathing is getting faster and faster. More and more irregular, until I get a stitch in my side and have to stop.

I put my weight on my thighs and try to breathe regularly. Exhausted, I flop onto the ground. I sit looking at the sea. It is so beautiful here, feeling the damp sand between my toes, the cool wind. I love the sea. I love being here, looking at the blue. Horizon and sea. All blue. I know we can't stay here for ever. Time is slipping away. In only a few days we'll leave. Back to reality. Back to life. Or what's left of it.

After my breathing has calmed a little, I look at the bottle in my hand. Think of what's in the letter. I wish so much that Toby could read it. There are so many things that I will never say to him.

I stand up and go a little way into the water. It's cold. I look at the bottle again, think of the words that are in it. Then I throw it as far out to sea as I can. The glass sparkles in the setting sun. Then the bottle disappears.

The last time I was at the sea I met my boyfriend. This time Mum is here. It's as if I've swapped my boyfriend for my mother. The time with Mum is lovely. It's lovely to have her again. But if it had been up to me, I'd have chosen Toby.

I laugh. I want it to sound like always. So that he won't notice. But it sounds artificial and put on. I'm trying not to look him in the eye. Otherwise he'll notice. I just want to have a nice evening and not think about the other stuff. Not about Dad. His trip. And Mum's card.

Toby comes over to me. Asks me something. No idea what. I force a smile and only look up briefly. Then he comes into my field of vision and lifts my chin with his finger. I try to avoid his look, but he's waiting for me to look at him. Only then does he say anything.

'Is everything all right? You've been so strange all evening.'

'Sure. Everything's fine,' I say.

'Have I done something wrong?'

I laugh at his question. It's not a nice laugh. 'Believe me, you're pretty much the only one in my life who doesn't do wrong things.'

He sighs and strokes back a lock of hair. Then he puts his arms around me. It does me good to be hugged.

'I don't understand you. Sometimes you are unfathomable. I try to work you out. But I can only do that if you let me get close.'

'I do.'

We go to the same school. I sleep with him at least two nights a week. We know everything about each other. What does he mean?

'Then tell me what's wrong.'

I shake my head. I don't want to. Not this evening.

Abruptly Toby lets me go. 'Well, leave it so.'

I can't stand it when he is angry.

'It's nothing. Really.'

'Then you tell me.'

'I don't want to spoil our evening.'

'It's already spoiled.'

I take a deep breath. 'Mum sent me a card. She hasn't appeared for two years. Only these ridiculous cards. I'm better off without her. I wish she'd get out of my life altogether and not just pop up when it suits her.'

It is really silly that I am letting the day be spoilt because of this. But it's too late now. I've said it. What'll Toby think now? What a touchy and moody girlfriend he has.

'You don't have to care. And even if your mother sent you a card every two weeks, she has no place in your life if you don't want that.'

What he says sounds so logical. But I can't change things. It has taken me two years to accept that I have no mother any more. I've pretended that she's dead. As far as I am concerned she is dead. If only there weren't these colourful postcards from all over the world.

'If Mum wouldn't send me anything that would prove she'd forgotten me. That would be easier for me.'

'Why?'

'Because then she wouldn't be thinking about me. I find it worse that she thinks about me but still stays away.'

Toby thinks. Then he says, 'You'd find it better if your mother forgot you? Because she loves her freedom more than you?'

I nod. Yes. He's understood it. Better than I do myself.

He puts his arms around me and it feels so unbelievably good. Calms me. Dries up the stupid tears that have started.

'Everyone needs their mother,' he whispers.

I pull away from him, so that I can look into his eyes. I stroke his cheek very slowly. Then I stand on tiptoe and kiss him.

'There you are.'

Mum comes towards me in the dark. She's holding a cardigan, which she hands to me.

She sits down beside me and together we look at the waves. 'Your father was worried.'

Your father was worried. She can't admit that she was. She has become a good friend. But I don't as a good mother. She's not the maternal type. Though maybe it's partly my fault. I'm not the daughter type either. I don't need a mother any more. I'm far too independent for that. I'm used to making my own decisions by myself. I muddle through. I don't need her as a mother.

All the same, it's bloody nice to lean on her shoulder.

Sometimes we have to realise that we are not perfect. That everything can't go perfectly and maybe that's OK. Maybe we don't have to function perfectly like machines to be able to live a perfect life. Maybe it's actually our little failings that make life worth living. It's OK to be the way you are. Because that's what makes us human.

We try to be perfect in all aspects of life. At school, in the family, at work, in our routines. Everything has to go according to plan. But if we accept that everything doesn't actually have to go according to plan, we can open up new possibilities. We don't have to plan all the time. We can just live. We have dreams, but we often postpone them. We forget that later may be too late. It's really easy to live life. We're the ones who make it complicated.

CHAPTER 21

All good things come to an end. We set off for home, and the closer we get, the more anxious I become. Suppose everything goes back to the way it was before the holiday? I wish the journey would never end. But eventually we arrive and I have to get out.

I long to be back at the seaside. I've imagined what it would be like just to stay there, to live in the little green house by the sea. It would be so lovely just to leave everything behind and start afresh.

At the sight of our house, a thousand moments with Toby and Joanne come tumbling back. I remember the time we made a cake. Toby and I had just got together and on this day, Joanne really gave him the once-over. She wanted to make sure that he really deserved me.

Oh, Joanne, she always watched out for me. She was the sensible one, made sure I kept my feet on the ground.

How I miss her! The hole in my heart hasn't got at all smaller. It's just as deep and dark as before the holiday.

'Will it never stop? Will it always hurt this much?'

Dr Frei looks right into my eyes as she answers. Her gaze is steady.

'Many people wish they could forget what they have experienced and to keep going the way they did before. If that's the way you are thinking, the answer has to be No. You will never be able to forget it. You will carry the scars for life. They will always hurt. But they will be a part of you. You will learn to live with this experience. And you will make new friendships.'

'I'll never be my old self again.'

Dr Frei shakes her head. 'You couldn't be that anyway. People change all the time, onwards and upwards. We grow through what we have experienced. Or it can break us. Whether you are going to grow or to break only you can decide.'

Not exactly encouraging words, you'll be thinking. All the same, it's the truth. I will never be my old self. I'll be a new person.

'I'm afraid that I may not like the person I am going to become.' And then I say something I've never told anyone. 'When I watched Toby die … I went empty inside. There is so much emptiness inside me. How can I ever fill it?'

Dr Frei passes me a handkerchief.

'I feel so guilty. I didn't help him. I didn't save him. I don't even know why. Why wasn't I beside him? Why did I just stand there in the corner?'

'Because at that moment you were not capable of it. You were in shock. Your brain couldn't properly process what it was seeing. And you wanted to live. Nobody blames you. Except yourself. You have to accept that you couldn't help Toby. And you have to forgive yourself for that.'

'And that will make the emptiness go away?'

Dr Frei gives me a cheering nod. 'Over time, it will. It's important to take it slowly, not to put yourself under pressure to feel good again. Healing takes time. And you have already made a lot of progress. Try out things that you might like. Meet your friends. Then you'll have good memories of Toby. You won't remember him with feelings of guilt. And regret.'

She gives me the address again of where the group therapy takes place. She thinks I should give it a try. I don't have to stay if I don't like it. I think it over. How would it be to go to a group session like that? Would it be like on TV? Would I have to stand up and introduce myself and tell what I have experienced? Though everyone knows that anyway. Maybe it's worth at try.

On the first Friday after the holidays, Dad, Mum and I go to the cinema. After the film, both my parents need to go to the loo. So I lean against the wall, waiting for them. I turn round when someone suddenly calls my name. I'm surprised to see Vanessa with a guy.

'Hey, what are you doing here?" I ask.

'Probably the same as you. Going to the movies.' She hugs me and points behind her: 'That's my cousin Stephen.'

I check out the boy behind her. About two or three years older than me and Vanessa, with dark brown eyes and dark blond hair.

'Hey, I'm Miriam.'

He nods. 'Vanessa talks about you a lot.'

'Oh, really?' I turn to her. 'You haven't said very much about your cousin.'

Vanessa shrugs. 'Really? Even so, Stephen and I have a pretty good relationship.'

I give her a meaningful grin and she shouts, 'No, not like that. That's *perverted*.'

Stephen gives her a nudge. 'I'm not all *that* ugly.'

No, he definitely is not. In fact, he's very good-looking. Not as good-looking as Toby … but not bad.

'I don't mean it like that. I mean, it would be as if I came on to my brother or something.' She turns back to me. 'Stephen is living with us at the moment because my mother is away on business. He's my babysitter. My mother is afraid I'll kill myself.'

When Vanessa realises what she has said, she looks at the floor, embarrassed. I feel exactly the same. Neither of us knows what to say.

Stephen saves the situation. 'I've heard about Joanne.

Vanessa told me that she was your best friend. I'm really sorry.'

If anyone else said something like that to me I'd be annoyed. After all, he didn't know her. But it sounds sincere coming from him.

At that moment Mum comes back and says, 'Oh, am I interrupting?'

'Not at all, Mum. This is Vanessa, a friend of mine, and this is her cousin Stephen.'

'Nice to meet you, Ma'am,' says Vanessa, holding out her hand to my mother like a well-brought up girl. 'Never had the opportunity before now.'

Wow, Vanessa, I love you. Absolutely polite, but got a dig in at Mum all the same.

Mum smiles. She knows exactly what Vanessa is getting at. And she takes it, because she knows it's true. 'No need to stand on ceremony,' she says.

Vanessa nods. Then she looks at the floor, embarrassed. Mum clears her throat. There's an awkward moment.

To break the silence, I say, 'My psychologist gave me the address of one of these group therapy sessions. Maybe you'd like to come too?'

Vanessa nods. 'What's it like?'

I shrug. 'Dunno. Haven't been there yet.'

She digs me with her elbow. 'So, you want me to go there and tell you what it's like. Is that it?'

'Like I always send you first into the crossfire.' I raise an eyebrow and make her laugh.

When I go on Facebook that evening, I have a friend request from Stephen. I click lazily through a few pages, till I land on Joanne's.

I look at pictures of the two of us. There were so many parties where we were photographed. We look so happy.

How can a thing just disappear? One bad thing follows another and before you know where you are, you're alone. Because everything you're used to, everything you take for granted, has disappeared out of your life. The very thought of going to some celebration or other!

I've changed so much. And Joanne too, before she ... killed herself. The sad truth is that it wouldn't make much difference if she were still alive. Because really she died on the day Mathias went berserk.

I scroll slowly over her Timeline. She's got dozens of posts in the past few weeks. Everywhere, people have written things like, I'm going to miss you. You were a very special person.

Tears fill my eyes and at the same time I'm getting angry. All these people didn't know Joanne properly. Not like I did.

They are right. Joanne was special. But how can they know that? They're just people from Joanne's music school or her sports club, who saw her once a week.

I don't really want to post anything. It feels stupid. Self-obsessed. After all, Joanne will never read any of the comments.

Only I have this feeling that I owe it to her. That I

should say goodbye to her. But everything sounds false. What should I post to her?

Then my gaze falls on the huge collage on my wall that Joanne and I made together. We put up lots of pictures of ourselves. And in the middle in big black letters on a white page is our motto.

Only Joanne would understand what it means. So it's perfect. My fingers are trembling as I start to type.

Her profile picture is staring at me. All that is to be seen is her head and shoulders. But I know how she looked that day. She was lying in the snow, wearing only leggings and a thick red jumper, her long dark hair spread out around her. We took new profile pictures of each other.

I sit on my bed, my laptop on my lap, and I start crying. Again. I remember that day so well. It was lovely.

We'll never have days like that ever again. She put an end to that. And I sit here alone on my bed without a best friend, without my boyfriend.

Some time maybe I will get another best friend. And a boyfriend too. But they will never be able to take Toby's and Joanne's places. They'll have new places. Toby's and Joanne's places will always be empty.

Slowly, I realise the sad truth. I will never stop crying for them. But it will get better. Maybe I'll be able to go a whole week without thinking of them. But the emptiness will never go away. In reality, you just get used to it. It becomes a part of you. You start to accept that that's the way life is. You're alone. You can't do anything about it.

On impulse, I write a note to Stephen. *I'm glad Vanessa has you. Thank you for looking after her.*

He's there for her, the way my mum is there for me. Maybe she's not such a bad mother as I used to think.

The next morning, I decide to give the group therapy a try. And that's how I come to enter the old building with peeling paint, looking for the room where my group meets.

It's not a big bare room like you see in the movies and there are no white-coated patients sitting around in a circle. It's a small room with big windows, which give it a bright, open feeling. There are some massive old bookcases around the walls. These contain some animal figures, board games, craft supplies and a few books. And there are hand-painted pictures, like in a kindergarten. A few school-kids are sitting at a round a table. I know a few of them to see.

A middle-aged man approaches me. He has an open smile.

'Hello. I'm Richard.' He puts out his hand to me.

Unsettled, I shake it. 'Miriam. I just wanted to see how group therapy works.'

Richard nods. 'You're always welcome.'

'My psychologist kept telling me so much about it that I really had no choice.'

Have I made a joke? I shake my head at myself.

Richard indicates an unoccupied chair. Then he turns

to the others. 'As you see, we have a new person from your school. Miriam would like to take a look at our group.'

Luckily, they don't all say in chorus, as they do in the movies, 'Hello, Miriam.' If they did, I'd have jumped up and run away.

Some of them say hello, others just nod at me.

I'm curious to check out the kids from my school who are sitting around the table. We're all about the same age. One of the girls speaks to me immediately.

'Hi. I'm Frederike. Have you been to group therapy before?'

I shake my head. I hadn't imagined it being like this at all. We're not sitting around in a circle. And if I listen to what's being said, most of them are not talking about the shooting.

'We're working with animals today,' says a boy. 'My name is Timo, by the way. We're supposed to choose one of the animal figures and explain why we are this animal. And then the others are supposed to choose an animal for you and explain why you are that animal.'

'The best thing is if you just listen at first,' says Richard, giving me an encouraging look, but without giving me the feeling that I'm in need of sympathy.

However, I don't really understand why we're supposed to compare ourselves to animals. It doesn't look like a kindergarten, but these are kindergarten *methods*.

'OK, Lisa, lets go,' calls Frederike, 'give me some animal names.'

It makes me want to laugh.

'OK,' says Lisa, thinking for a moment. She pushes her hair back and then she takes the deer. 'I'm a deer, because I'm bloody scary. And I'm running away from everything.'

Her hands are playing tentatively with the animal. I think it costs her quite an effort to speak her mind like this.

The boy beside her shakes his head. I know him by sight. He reaches for an animal. 'I think you're more a cat.' The boy seems relaxed. He looks straight at Lisa and speaks without hesitation. I'd never have guessed he'd witnessed the shooting. He seems so normal. But maybe it's just a façade. 'You're careful, that's true. But even so, you approach people and you're curious about what's happening around you.'

A third girl speaks up. She's called Corinne. She used to be in Toby's class. I've spoken to her a few times, but not since the shooting. She is also of the opinion that Lisa is a cat.

Timo chooses a swan for Lisa, because he finds that she is often unapproachable. Then Lisa starts to explain why *he* could be a swan, rather than her. And Frederike compares him to a vulture, because he pounces on everything. They are starting to get louder and they aren't saying only nice things about each other but at the same time they don't seem to be nasty.

Corinna notices my rather puzzled expression. She

gives me a smile. She's not like she was before, when Toby was still alive. She's changed too.

'You know, we always talk like this to each other,' she whispers to me. 'It wasn't always like this, but now we've known each other for a few months, and I'm really starting to look forward to the sessions.'

During the conversation, I find out that the other boy is called Daniel. He always says what he thinks and comes across as extremely self-confident. But he's nice all the same. Everyone is agreed that he is a meerkat. He always has a joke on the go and he's relaxed.

I don't feel bad at all. Maybe I even feel quite good in this company. I had expected that I was going to have to talk about the shooting, but none of them are doing that. Sometimes they are distracted from their task and talk about other things entirely. Normal things.

At the end of the session, everyone in the group says I absolutely have to come again. I think I probably will. It's not bad at all. I start towards my bus-stop, smiling. It will come right. Gradually I'll get hold of my life again. I'm going to make it.

People are rushing by, pushing past me, but I'm sauntering along. In the commotion of the shopping area of town, a face comes towards me, a face I recognise. The woman is wearing a trouser suit and pumps. Her brown bob frames her narrow face. She's wearing the same pointy glasses as before. She's hardly changed. Only her cheeks seem to have sunk. She's got thinner.

'Tatjana.' I stop in front of her and look in surprise at Toby's mother.

She looks up and widens her eyes. 'Miriam.' Her lips form my name, but she says it so softly that I can't hear it.

I open my mouth and close it again. I don't know what to say. We haven't seen each other for three months. Since then so much has happened.

Even though she is a very tall woman, she looks unsure of herself, almost lost. I give a start. 'I couldn't go to his funeral. It just wasn't possible.'

I shake my head sadly. Tatjana and I have made instant contact.

'You're nervous,' says Toby with a laugh. We're standing outside his front door. I give him a foul look. I can't keep my hands still. I'm rocking back and forth on the soles of my feet.

'Do you find it funny?' I scrunch up my eyes. 'There's nothing worse than if your boyfriend's mother can't stand you.'

He pulls me close and ruffles my hair.

Well, that's just great. I've gone to the trouble of curling my hair and now he's messing up my hairstyle. I might as well have come without combing my hair. I don't want to make a bad impression on his parents.

'They will love you. Don't worry.' And then he unlocks the door and we're into the lion's den.

I have no idea how I should behave. What should I talk to his parents about?

'Mama? Papa? I've brought someone home.' He takes me by the hand and steers me through a narrow hallway into the living room. 'I've told you about Miriam.'

The two people who are watching television look up at the sound of my name. They turn towards me with friendly smiles.

'Hello, Miriam. I'm Tatjana.' She puts out her hand.

'Paul.' His father winks at me and offers me his hand.

I shake each hand in turn and try to smile.

'You should have warned us, Toby.' Tatjana chides her son. 'Now your girlfriend is going to get the wrong impression about us.' She turns back to me. 'We don't normally spend the whole day watching the box. If I'd known you were coming I'd have baked a cake.'

I hold up the plastic bag in my left hand. 'I've brought cake.' My voice doesn't sound exactly confident. *Get a grip, Miriam.*

'Well, in that case.' His mother takes the cake from me. 'Welcome to the family.'

'Same with me. I didn't know whether it would be OK with you if I rang you. After all that happened ...' She makes a helpless gesture with her hands as if she wanted to emphasise the *After all that happened* … 'I'd have understood if you wanted to cut yourself off from the past.'

I shake my head. 'I just didn't know what I should say because … well …'

How can I say to her that I have been feeling guilty about Toby's death? That this feeling of guilt has still not fully gone away?

'Have you time for a cup of coffee?' I ask.

'Love to.'

In a little side street, away from the hustle and bustle, we find a quiet and comfortable little café. The spring sun shines on the small round tables. We decide to sit outside. The noise of the crowds is quite muffled here.

I smile nervously at Tatjana. 'What I wanted to say …' I close my eyes briefly to get my words in order. 'I was there. I saw him lying on the floor.'

I squint and look at my fingernails.

'Oh, Miriam. I didn't know that.' She touches my hand, then gives it a sympathetic squeeze. But I don't want her sympathy. She doesn't understand.

My voice faltering, I say, 'I was there and I didn't do anything to help him. I just stood there by the door and watched.'

I don't dare to look at her. How will she react? I really like Toby's mother. She treated me as if I was her child too. She mothered me. It was lovely. Because I didn't get that at home, and I can't tell her how grateful I am.

Instead I have to tell her such a dreadful thing.

At that moment the waiter comes and asks if we've decided what we'd like. Tatjana orders a café latte and I just ask for the same as her.

When the waiter is gone, the whole world seems quiet. Tatjana doesn't say anything. I look up carefully and stare straight into a pair of eyes that are just like Toby's. And I know this facial expression also from him.

'Do you blame yourself?' She shakes her head incredulously. 'You couldn't have done anything to save him. Nobody blames you.' She gives me a penetrating look.

I scratch at the wood of the table. My hands need to be doing something.

'Nobody but Mathias Staudt is to blame,' she says suddenly.

Surprised at these hard words, I look at her for a moment. Then I shake my head.

'It wasn't all his fault. I wonder what it must have been like inside his head that he was able to do such a terrible thing. Sometimes, I feel almost sorry for him. Even though at the same time he will always be a monster for me.'

Only when I say it do I realise that it is true. His life must really have been terrible for all those years. That doesn't justify going on a shooting spree, but I still think that we can't blame just him for what happened. But I'd never said that before.

'How do you mean?' Tatjana gives me a puzzled look.

I shrug, because I don't know how to put my thoughts into words. 'Since Toby's death, I have thought a lot about it all. About how we treated Mathias. We were really mean to him. But you can probably only understand if you were there.'

The waiter bringing our coffee interrupts our conversation. Tatjana takes a sip, but I just stir the milky foam around with my spoon. She thinks I shouldn't blame myself. That is such a huge relief. If even Toby's mother doesn't blame me, then maybe I've got it wrong. Nobody seems to expect that I should have put my life on the line for Toby.

'I really don't understand it,' says Tatjana softly. 'How can you say such a thing, even though you were there?'

Well, how can I? I have no answer. This attitude has developed slowly, by stealth, over the months. Mathias shot seven teachers and pupils. He is a murderer. He made the decision himself to do what he did. The logical conclusion is that I should hate him. But I don't. Or at least, I don't only hate him.

CHAPTER 22

In my dream I'm back at the sea. The sea in Spain. I'm lying with Toby on the beach. But then his face distorts and Toby changes into Mathias Staudt. He puts his hands to my throat, drags me to the water and dunks my head underwater again and again. I can't breathe. The salt water is burning my lungs. Then I drown.

I open my eyes and take deep breaths. Only a dream. I can breathe. A glance at the alarm clock tells me that it's only 23.26.

I know there is no point in even trying to get back to sleep. So I turn on the light, grab my laptop and let it boot up as I make tea in the kitchen.

I sit cross-legged on my bed with my laptop open, a cup of camomile tea beside me. On Facebook, I see that Stephen is online. I'm just thinking about contacting him when a message suddenly appears from him: *So, still awake?*

I type back: *Yes, couldn't sleep. How about you?*

Stephen writes: *Vanessa shouted out in her sleep. She's*

213

OK now, but just to be on the safe side, I'm sitting with her for a while.

I know that Vanessa sleeps badly too. She's told me that. But I envy her that she has someone to look after her.

I write: *Good that she's not alone.*

Stephen writes: *It's terrible to hear her shouting. I always feel so useless, because I don't know how to help her.*

I smile. An outright foolish grin. I find it so sweet that he's concerned about his cousin. I have no siblings or cousins.

I write: *She's lucky to have you.*

I don't know if anyone has ever said that to him before. If not, it's high time someone did. I've no idea whether Stephen is still at school or at college or works. Anyway, he has his own life, and to be looking after someone as fucked up as Vanessa and I are takes time and energy.

Anyone would do it, comes a new message.

I roll my eyes. Why can't guys ever accept compliments? *Yeah, sure.*

Stephen writes: *Have you nobody to stay with you?*

Even if I had someone, I wouldn't allow it. The only person I'd allow to comfort me would be Toby. Or Joanne, of course. But neither of them will ever comfort me again.

Not exactly. I don't write any more than that. Stephen mustn't know how things are with me. He has enough on his hands with Vanessa.

What about your parents?

I don't know if I shout out in my sleep, but nobody has ever come to me in the night.

They don't notice.

It's a while before I get an answer to that.

I'd say they'd come if you asked them.

Now I'm the one who has to think for a moment before I write back: *Have you got helping syndrome or what? I think looking after one girl is enough …;)*

Then Stephen writes: *Vanessa has told me about your mum. She's come back, just because of you. So she'd get up in the night for you too.*

I'm a bit taken aback. I tell him I'm going back to bed, tell him goodbye and log out.

Mum. She's part of my life now. But why? Because I really love her, or just because I need someone to cling to at the moment? But I do think I'm going to get better. At some stage, I won't need anyone to cling to. Will she go off again then? Or will she stick around? Can she really become my mother again?

The next day, Vanessa is sick. Probably she's so exhausted from her sleepless night that she just needs a bit of peace.

All the same, I start to panic. The last time Joanne didn't come to school, she never came again. So I drop by to Vanessa's after school with our homework. I tell myself I'm just doing it so that she doesn't miss out on school.

Which is total rubbish. I'm checking up on her.

Stephen opens the door, his hair tousled, his eyes sleepy. 'Miriam, come in.'

'I just wanted to know how Vanessa is.'

'Not so good. She developed a fever during the night. That was a bit much for me. I rang my mother. She came round and told me what to do. She stayed until I got back from school. Now she's gone to the hospital. She's on duty. And I feel totally useless.'

He seems helpless. I feel really sorry for him. So I touch him on the arm. 'You're doing great. What I wrote last night, I meant it. She's lucky to have you.'

'Nonsense.' Stephen seems embarrassed.

I have to suppress a grin. Typical boy!

I make for Vanessa's room, but Stephen holds onto my hand.

'Miriam, I'm sorry if I said anything hurtful last night. Or annoyed you. Or whatever. But you didn't log out of Facebook because you were tired. I wrote the wrong thing. I don't know what it was. But I'm really sorry.'

'You didn't write anything wrong. It's just that it reminded me that there's something I have to sort out for myself.'

I open Vanessa's door a crack. She's lying in bed, her eyes closed. She's asleep. I slip into the room and close the door behind me. I pull a chair up quietly to her bed and sit down beside her.

She looks so fragile. Her wavy brown hair is plastered

to her head, her face is flushed with fever, her lips are dry. She must be feeling horrible.

I root in my bag for the homework and leave it on the desk. Then I watch her sleeping. Watch how her chest rises and falls with each breath. She's alive. Not like Joanne. She's not going to kill herself.

Still, I can feel the fear. Suppose I lost Vanessa too? That would be too much. But I'm not going to lose her. She's going to stay, at least for now. But what will happen next hear or in five years' time, nobody can tell.

After a while, I slink out of the room again. Stephen is playing X-box in the living room. I come into his line of vision, but in such a way as not to block his view of the screen. I'm trying to push the noises into the background.

'I'm off, so. I've left Vanessa's homework. She doesn't have to do it if she doesn't want to.'

Stephen is still staring at the screen. Then he finally pauses the game and looks at me. 'No problem.' He sounds tired and distant.

'Everything all right?'

'Yep.'

I know this kind of behaviour with guys. They sound like this when they have a problem and they don't want to admit it.

'Well, bye so.' And before he can answer, I'm gone.

At home, I meet my mother. She wants to know why I'm

so late home from school and I throw a hissy fit. I throw myself onto my bed. Listen to music. Get my homework over with. Not very well. Who cares?

It's all getting me down. This whole boring routine. My mother, who is so touchingly concerned about me. This normality. But it's not one bit normal. This is no life. This is just an outer shell of me that just keeps going, somehow.

Linkin Park is buzzing in my ears. 'Valentine's Day'. One of my favourite songs. Suits my mood. Just like the weather. Clouds are gathering. The sky is getting dark, though it's still afternoon. My window is open and there's a sharp wind. It's going to rain.

I feel out of sorts. Tired. All washed up. Totally exhausted. As if I'm sickening for something. Only I'm not sickening for anything.

But the heartless wind kept blowing, blowing. Yes, I love this song. The tune, the lyrics, the rhythm, the powerful ending. Absolutely brilliant. On an impulse, I run downstairs, slip into my Vans, pull on my denim jacket and scoot. To the cemetery.

Today I'm visiting Joanne. Her mother has planted the grave so beautifully with flowers, pink and yellow. Sadly I read her name on the gravestone. Over and over again. How easily things can just slip away. Joanne and I had no idea.

Shortly before the end of the second period, I get a text from Toby. I sneak a look at it.

What are you doing
this evening. Maths
is so boring. Miss you.
Toby

Joanne reads it over my shoulder and gives me a dig. 'Forget it. We've agreed to do something together this evening. Your sweetheart can take a back seat.'

That's true. Joanne and I were planning to have a pizza and borrow a couple of films

I text him back:

Sry. Can't. Otherwise
will be eaten by monsters.

'Monsters? Well, thanks a bunch.' Joanne pretends to be insulted.

'Oh, come on! You know I love you the best. I bow humbly. I kiss your cheek.'

'Eeew! Joanne and Miriam are lesbians!' cries Marcus from the row behind us.

Some of the class yell '*What?*' Others say, 'Rubbish!' and the rest just laugh.

'Really. Miriam just kissed Joanne. I saw!'

'Knew it all along.' Patrick gives a satisfied grin.

'I dunno. Do they *look* lesbian?' Pia is asking Greta, who *is* lesbian. She came out a year back. Nobody gives a damn, except for a few boys who fancied her.

'I don't know,' Greta says, considering. 'Miriam is hot. But I'm not so sure about Joanne.'

I throw a folder at her. The whole class is laughing.

'If I were lesbian,' says Joanne, 'I think I'd have better taste than to get mixed up with Miriam.'

More laughter and yelling. Then Greta stands up, takes my face in her hands and kisses me on the cheek, just like I kissed Joanne.

'Miriam, you slut. Two girls on one day. You should be ashamed of yourself,' Patrick calls out and gives Marcus a high five.

Frau Klaas tries in vain to bring the class under control. 'Quiet! Silence, please. I don't care who kisses who, but please, not in my class.' Frau Klaas is giving us the evil eye. But you can tell that she's enjoying the fun.

Joanne and I are chortling. Us and the rest of the class. 'I'm telling Toby,' someone shouts, and with that total mayhem breaks out.

The bell rings for break. The others all run out. Joanne and I are practically rolling on the floor with the giggles.

Frau Klaas gives her watch an impatient glance. 'Off with you, the pair of you. Or I'll have to lock you in here.'

Joanne and I stumble, laughing, out of the classroom, hardly able to keep upright.

'Oh, man, Patrick is …'

Boom!

'What was that?'

People around us are starting to screech. I can see Philip running. And then I realise what I've just heard.

Everything was so normal. Until just that moment. The moment just before that gave no hint of what was to come. Nothing warns us. We have no time to say goodbye. We could never for a second have thought what was going to happen. And that's exactly how it should be. If we were to think about all the dangers, if we'd always known what was going to happen at that moment, we'd have lived our whole lives in fear.

At any time, anything can knock us back. But it doesn't actually happen very often. Statistics are of no use. Either it happens to you or it doesn't. And if it does happen to you – well, you're out of luck. And if nothing happens, then you're dead lucky, only you don't know it.

A thunderclap startles me. The dark clouds suddenly open. The rain comes streaming at me. And it feels good.

The next day, there's still no sign of Vanessa at school. I stick it out as long as the fourth period, and then I grab my things and skedaddle. I'm not a fan of bunking off school, but I can't stand it any longer. I feel better as soon as I get outside. Fresh air. No bad-tempered teachers. No Spanish class.

I wander around aimlessly. Pass shops. Arrive in a residential area. Pedestrians of all sorts, dogs and their masters, mothers and their babies, old people with their carers – they're all coming in my direction.

A police car drives past me. But I'm lucky. The driver doesn't stop to ask why I'm not at school.

I arrive eventually at our garden gate. I've come home to my mum. I just hug her, without warning. Totally surprised, she returns the hug.

'I was cross with you for so long. So angry, because you'd just left. And I've often wondered if I could simply forgive you.'

I notice my mother stiffening. 'And what conclusion have you reached?'

'I don't know. You're here now. You came when I needed help. Maybe you'll go away again some time. But for the moment you're here.'

Mum hugs me close. 'I'll always come back. It will never again be like the last time. I promise. I've learnt from my mistakes.'

'I know,' I whisper, keeping back the tears. It will hurt when she goes. But she will have to do it. That's her life. But she'll be back. She'll be there for me. And that's what counts.

CHAPTER 23

In the middle of May, Vanessa and I decide to go shopping. We used to do that all the time. But in recent months, we haven't given much thought to clothes. Now it's a bit strange. Every second thing we look at makes us want to cry, because it would have suited Joanne, Sophia or Tanja.

After Vanessa and I have visited about twenty shops, and have accumulated a pretty respectable stash of stuff, we take a break, go into a nice café and order huge ice-creams. We order a scoop of every flavour – and there are about twenty of them. We'll never manage it all, but it doesn't matter. It's a tradition, something that we used to do when we were together, all five. And traditions shouldn't be abandoned.

'I love this ice-cream,' murmurs Vanessa, shovelling a huge spoon of it into her mouth.

'Would you like me to use this phone app I've got to work out how many calories that makes?'

Vanessa shoots me a deadly look. 'Don't care. I don't mind putting on the weight.'

'Because you can just eat what you want and stay slim all the same.'

'Yeah. Fate. There are people like me who can eat what they like, and there are people like you who just go to pieces.'

'There are people like you who have to be thin in order to be pretty, and there are people like me, who are just attractive anyway.'

We laugh at our ridiculous comments. It feels good to behave so normally.

'Do you know who you've made a lasting impression on in spite of your bad figure?' She gives me a wink.

'Not a clue.' I give her a surprised look.

'My cousin.'

'Stephen?'

'Mmm. The poor boy can't stop talking about you.' Vanessa stuffs another spoonful into her mouth. 'I've been trying to work out for days what you've done to fascinate him.'

'You think Stephen likes me?' I raise an eyebrow. 'I mean, in *that* way?'

'Yep. I'm absolutely sure of it.'

Oh. I mean, oh. 'I haven't thought about anything like that since ...' I leave the rest of the sentence hanging in mid-air. Vanessa knows what I mean.

'I don't mean you should throw yourself at him. But life is going on all around us.' Vanessa touches my hand. 'Toby can't be the only boy in your life for ever. Because he's not there. Stephen is. I just want you to think about it. If you don't *like* Stephen, that's different.'

'Stephen is nice, as far as I can judge.' I don't want to say that it feels like a betrayal.

'I don't want to spoil your day, Miriam. Just think it over.'

'Are you trying to tell me that I can only live if I have a guy?' I give her a challenging look. I certainly don't want to mess up the day. 'Because if that's the case, we'd better find one for you pretty quickly.'

Vanessa smiles at me over the ice-cream. 'No need. I've met someone.'

'No!' I give a broad grin.

'Yes.' Vanessa is beaming. 'He's called Mike. We met just two weeks ago. I didn't want to say anything, because I didn't know how you'd react.'

'How I'd react? I'm delighted for you. What else would you expect?'

She tucks a stray lock of hair nervously behind her ear. 'I don't really know.'

Vanessa is right. All around us, everyone else is getting on with life. We have to get on with it too. I can't get Vanessa's words out of my head. They bother me all week. I keep thinking how it would be if I let a boy get close to me again. And if that boy were Stephen.

Damn. Why did Vanessa tell me that? I don't want

any guy in my life. I'm glad just to be able to get up in the morning without being afraid. I'm happy about every baby step that I can take. This would be a giant step, though.

I used to discuss everything with Joanne. She always had something sensible to say. And even though I know she can't answer me, I go to the cemetery and sit by her grave.

I can just imagine what she would say to me. It's almost as if I can hear her. *What's wrong, Miri? You look as if the world is coming to an end. It can't be that bad.*

'It's all so complicated, Joanne. I don't know what to do. There's this boy who fancies me. And he seems to be really nice.'

If she could answer me, she'd say, *So what's the problem?*

And I'd explain to her, I'm not sure if I'm ready. If I can let Toby go. And if I can't, then that wouldn't be fair on Stephen.

But Joanne isn't here. She will never answer me again, and I will never be able to tell her my problems.

Perhaps it would all have come about differently if I hadn't gone to the group session the following week. As it happens, we were to discuss what we thought of the topic of friendship and partnership.

I sit with Lisa, Corinna, Frederike and Daniel. Lisa

says she's broken up with her boyfriend, because since the shooting all they've done is fight. Neither of them approved of the way the other had behaved.

Timo only got to know his girlfriend because of the shooting. She's a nurse and she treated him after the shooting. It did him good to talk to her and they ended up getting together.

At first of course I don't want to say anything. What has it to do with the others? But in the end I remember how good I always feel after I've talked.

'There's this guy who likes me. And I think he's very nice. But to like him feels like a betrayal of Toby. We never broke up, and that makes me feel I'd be going behind his back.'

I cross my arms. I'd never have thought I'd ever talk about a thing like this.

'For sure, your boyfriend wouldn't have wanted you to hide away from the world. So if you like this guy, it's actually betraying your boyfriend if you *don't* get to know him better.' Corinna smiles at me as she says that.

Well, it's something to think about.

'You shouldn't expect too much of yourself,' Frederike says. 'When you're ready, you'll know.'

Daniel gets right to the heart of it. 'You're just afraid of losing someone else. But that is going to happen anyway in your life. Don't you want to be as happy as you can, while you can?'

That hit home. Direct. And pretty true. Of course I'm afraid of being hurt again.

Stephen is totally different from Toby. Toby was always easygoing and kept his cool. As far as I can tell, Stephen and I would be well able to fight. I talked a lot with Toby. We had a lot in common. No matter what the story was with me, he always knew. And we messed around a lot. Stephen is more the silent type.

I really should get to know him better, and one thing is sure: I shouldn't compare the two of them like that. That's not fair.

Everyone has their own story. Not just my life has been changed. Others' lives too. I've given up fighting these thoughts. The shooting has changed me.

Nothing stays the same. We learn that as we grow up. We can't hold onto anything. Not even ourselves. We make our way through life and we keep leaving people behind. Very few accompany us throughout our whole lives. I think that's the hardest thing. To be alone. Of course there are people who can help, but everyone is really alone in life.

CHAPTER 24

Right, well, it's not such a big thing. I'm going to calm down and ring the bell. It's not so hard. All I have to do is give a nice smile and ask Stephen if he'd like to go to the park with me. In this lovely weather, normal people all go to the park and lie on the grass.

Damnation! Why am I making such a big deal of it? It's not even a proper date. Even so, I feel panicky. This is not what I want. I'm not ready.

Stop, I order myself, *don't give up now. Why shouldn't I give him a chance? If it's awful, then I never have to see him again. And if I feel I have a bad conscience because of Toby, well, I can just finish it.*

I press the bell quickly.

My palms are damp. I pray that Stephen won't answer the door. And at the same time, I know I'll be disappointed if that's the way it is.

There isn't a sound for several seconds. I breathe out, relieved. It's a stupid idea. I'm just about to turn around when sounds come from the house. Feet on the stairs. Children shouting.

Oh no! Damn!

The front door opens and a girl of about three stands there. She has blond ringlets and freckles. She has an ice-cream in her hand. She stares at me, her mouth open.

I haven't much experience with small children. I give her a smile, hoping she's not going to scream and run away. '

'Hi! Is Stephen in?'

Just at that moment he comes out of the kitchen. When he sees me, he gives a surprised grin.

'Miriam, what are you doing here?'

He picks the little girl up in his arms.

'Am I disturbing you? I came because … because I thought …' And of course, now I come to think of it, it seems completely stupid to ask him if he'd like to go to the park. We don't even know each other properly. 'Eh … maybe you'd like to hang out a bit with me? Y'know, spend a bit of time together?'

Oh, shit. Can the earth please, please just open up and swallow me? Now. That is such rubbish that I'm talking. I can't. I don't want to.

'What's your name?' The little girl is looking at me curiously. I feel quite uncomfortable, the way she's peering at me.

'Miriam. And you?'

'Alisa. But your hair is a funny colour.' She sticks a finger in her mouth.

'Really?' I ask, amused. She's really cute. 'Your hair

is gorgeous, though, don't you think?' Then I turn to Stephen and ask. 'Is this your sister?'

'My half-sister. I have a half-brother too. And an older sister, who's left home.'

Three siblings. Four children. Oh my God! Out loud, I say, 'That's a lot.'

Stephen shrugs his shoulders. 'Well, there's always something going on around here anyway. Especially with the two small ones.'

'I'm not small. I'm four,' Alisa protests, insulted. She struggles until Stephen puts her down.

'You're right. Of course you're a big girl. Don't mind your silly brother.'

Alisa laughs. A sweet laugh, free, unforced.

'Please don't talk nonsense to my sister.' Stephen isn't really cross, he's just playing along.

'Why? I'm just telling the truth.' I bat my eyelashes.

Alisa laughs again. Then a woman's voice calls her and she disappears.

I feel uncomfortable again, out of place. It wasn't a good idea to come. Stephen clearly hasn't any time.

'Eh, I'm sorry. I think I'm in the way. It's better if I just leave.'

I'm about to turn when Stephen stops me. 'You're not in the way at all.'

I give him a doubtful look. But he gives such an uncertain smile, it makes me feel better. He doesn't know any more than I do what's happening here.

So I lift up my basket, which has a blanket flopping out of it. 'I was hoping you might come to the park with me.'

The sun warms my face. I lie on my back on the blanket and pull at a few blades of grass. Stephen is sitting next to me, his arms around his knees. We've been chattering for an hour about all kinds of things. Family, school, pastimes. Stephen likes football.

What a surprise! A man who likes football! He realised at once that I know as much about it as the average tomato.

'If you could relive a particular day, which one would you choose?'

Stephen gives me a surprised look. He thinks for a while and then he says. 'The day I went to Dresden with my father and stepmother and my brother and sisters to my grandparents' golden wedding anniversary.'

'Why?'

'That was the first time I felt as if we were a family. When my father first met Kathrine, after the divorce, I felt for a long time that we were a crazy mixed-up lot. That was the first day we were really all together. But why did you want to know?'

I close my eyes and turn my face to the sun. 'I don't know. I just want to get to know you better.'

Maybe I've gone too far? But when I throw him a quick glance, I see that I haven't. Stephen is beaming.

'And what have you found out about me so far?'

'I think you're a home bird. You love to have a bit of turmoil going on around you. You need to have people around. I can just see you in twenty years' time, living in a house in the suburbs, with at least three children.'

'Scary. Are you clairvoyant?'

I give a giggle. 'Sure. My crystal ball is at the bottom of my basket.'

'So you don't believe in fate.'

'No-o. Life ...' I'm searching for the right words. '... just happens. Nobody can control it.'

I sigh. I'm feeling sad again, though I've promised myself I'm going to be a fifteen-year-old girl.

'That's nothing to be ashamed of, Miriam.'

I open my eyes and turn on my side so I can see him better. 'What do you mean?'

Stephen smiles and tucks a stray hair behind my ear. This touch affects me so much that I can't speak.

'Vanessa is the same. At one moment she is happy, and then suddenly it hits her all over again. That's part of how you both are. But it seems you want to hide that from everyone.'

We are looking right into each other's eyes, without looking away, without embarrassment. It's one of those moments of total honesty between two people.

'It has nothing to do with embarrassment. It's just that it makes things a bit easier if you can act for a few hours as if the shooting never happened.'

'Vanessa doesn't talk about it.'

'It's just that it's hard to talk to outsiders about it.' I turn onto my back and let the afternoon sun shine on me.

'I'm not an outsider.'

'In this context, you are. Pretty well everyone is.'

Neither of us says anything more. But it is not a painful silence. There is nothing more to say. For the moment.

It's getting gradually cooler. The sun will be going down soon. I love this time of day. Everything gets quiet. There are fewer cars on the road. The birds are twittering. Most people are leaving the park. A cat mews somewhere. And muffled voices are to be heard from far off. At this time of day, I sometimes get the feeling that everything is good again. I feel lighter. I have the feeling the world is spinning a bit more slowly.

Peace, everything seems to say. *Peace. Take deep breaths.*

'What are you thinking?' Stephen is looking curiously at me.

'I'm thinking now nice it is just to be here, doing nothing.'

'So you're not one for hustle and bustle?'

I shrug. 'I used to be like that. What I'm like now – I don't really know.'

'You'll work that out some time.'

'Possibly. But even if I don't, it's no big deal. I am who I am. That's enough.

'You're a survival artist.'

'What?' I ask, taken aback. I don't know what he's driving at.

'It's the first word that comes to mind to describe you. Survival artist. You take life as it comes. You are a survival artist. You adapt to the situation.'

'Hm. I don't feel a bit like that,' I say.

'Well, that's how it appears to me.'

'Then I'm a good actress.' Now I'm whispering. We've hit a topic that I'm not so keen to discuss.

Stephen shrugs his shoulders. 'People don't see themselves as others see them.'

'People see themselves as they are.' I contradict him.

'People are as they behave. And another person can judge that better than oneself. Me, for example.' Stephen gives me an encouraging grin. He's trying to cheer me up. And it's working.

'You're sweet.' I lean forward and kiss him on the cheek.

He goes bright red. I suddenly think of Toby.

'I really ought to go. It's late.' I stand up.

What a stupid thing to say! I don't want to mix Stephen and Toby up. It's not fair to Stephen. But that is exactly what is going to happen. I'm always going to compare the two of them.

Stephen gives me a puzzled look. But I can't explain it to him. So he won't feel that he's done something wrong, I add, 'That was the best day I've had for ages. If I had to choose a day to relive since the shooting, it would be this one with you.' And that's the truth.

Toby is breathing behind me. On my back, I can feel his chest rising and falling. When we sleep over in his parents' mobile home, I sometimes stay awake just to feel him. I don't really think, just feel. Until I drift off.

At the beginning, I couldn't sleep because it was a new and somehow rare feeling to lie naked with a guy. I did learn to sleep like that. In fact, those nights I spend with Toby, I slept best.

But even better than falling asleep is waking up. At moments like that I feel beautiful and invincible. This morning, I wake up because the mattress moves and I miss the heat at my back. Toby is getting up.

I turn over quickly and pull him back into bed. I lay my head on his chest and give him a wide smile. 'Where are you going?'

Toby pulls my head towards him by two long locks of hair in order to kiss me briefly. 'To make breakfast for my girlfriend.'

I give an evil giggle. 'I've trained you well.'

Toby grabs me by the wrists, pushes me back against the mattress and half lies on top of me. 'So it would appear.'

He kisses me again, this time hotter and hungrier. As far as I am concerned, we could take this a bit further, but

Toby lets go of me and this time he's so quick, I can't stop him. He grabs his boxer shorts and pulls them on.

I cock my head. 'What are you doing now?'

'Baking bread rolls.'

'It seems I've trained you too well.'

I remember that weekend so well. It was two weeks before the shooting. Everything was so perfect. I'd never have thought it would all be over between us.

It hurts so much to think about him. I can't imagine that it will ever stop hurting. Not totally. Some people say you never forget your first love.

In the next few days, Stephen tries three times to reach me. I don't answer. I send him a text to say I have no time just at the moment.

On one of these days, I have an appointment with Dr Frei. I'm more closed than usual and that doesn't go unnoticed. She leaves me in peace for a while before she asks me about it.

'I've got to know a boy. But he reminds me all the time of Toby.' A few months ago, I'm not so sure if I'd have told her a thing like that.

'Because they are so alike?' Dr Frei's voice is kind but firm. I've often wondered how she does it. She never has a bad day and always looks relaxed.

'Not really. I like Stephen. I can be myself with him. For him, the shooting is part of my life. He doesn't put pressure on me to talk about it, but if I do talk about it, it doesn't do his head in. The only thing is that I keep comparing him with my dead boyfriend. And that's not fair.'

There's another reason too. I wonder if I should mention it. But of course Dr Frei has already realised that there is something more, and she gives me an encouraging look.

'Toby would always have been my first choice. I wouldn't have bothered with Stephen before. Stephen is some boy that I might just fall in love with. Toby is the boy for me.'

It was a stupid idea to meet Stephen. Toby is *the* boy, and the only reason he isn't is that he's dead. Gone.

'That can change. Another boy could be the boy.'

'And where does that leave Toby? He's my ex? Or just nobody?'

We go on living through the people who go on thinking about us. I don't believe in resurrection or in life after death. For me, people live on by being thought of. That's a kind of immortality.

If I don't think about Toby, then who will? Who'll remember the good times and go on loving him? And how can you substitute another for someone that you have loved so much? Indian women who have lost their husbands set candles on the Ganges, to remember their husbands by. That's a lovely ritual. That way, they are never fully forgotten. But how can I make sure Toby is not forgotten?

When you are small, you can't wait to be grown up. When I was in the playground, I used to look admiringly at the groups of older girls who wore cool gear, laughed, smoked, drank beer. They were always so self-confident.

When I got to be ten, twelve, I was really looking forward to becoming a girl like that. But as time went by, I began to realise that there was more to it than clothes and cool turns of phrase. It didn't take me long to twig that smoking is disgusting and that most guys only want the one thing. I had problems with my father, my friends, boys. The parties were not always as great as they had looked to me. It's mostly about drinking. One guy turns into an idiot, the other one just gets embarrassing and it ends with everyone puking.

From then on, I wanted one thing above all. To feel like a kid again, even if only for a few hours. To feel free, unconstrained, naïve. To be simple, without responsibilities or complicated thoughts.

Then I met Toby and I discovered that there was something really beautiful about being grown-up. Toby showed me that you can get something even when everything familiar disappears.

Now Toby is dead, and that's something familiar gone. And that hurt terribly, and still hurts.

If I were to start something with Stephen, how long would it be before he would disappear, which would hurt all over again?

At some stage, one or other of us would end the relationship. I mean, what is the probability of finding the great love of your life at fifteen? Very, very small.

'What is it that you are really afraid of, Miriam?'

'How do you mean?'

'Think about these things. Are these problems really there, or are you creating them yourself so that you don't have to face the truth?

A few months ago, I'd have exploded if someone spoke to me like that.

So what do I want?

And what do I not want?

Maybe I should start to think about the future, to lay plans again. And one question that won't go away is this: Do I want Stephen to be part of these plans?

Yes or no.

We have to make decisions. We can't always hide away. We have to live. That's why we're here. That's the only real reason.

CHAPTER 25

'Hey, Mike, give me one of those.'

A beer bottle comes flying through the air and I catch it.

'You shouldn't throw things to her. She has no motor skills. The only good catch she ever made was me.' Stephen gives a grin.

'You're going to catch it in a minute,' I say, threatening him with the beer bottle as Vanessa comes out of the house with a bowl of salad.

'You should give that fellow his walking papers. Since you two got together he's become insufferably smug.' She gives a wink.

I roll my eyes. 'And there was I thinking he would be nice and quiet.'

Mike laughs. Vanessa shakes her head. And Stephen is grinning from ear to ear.

'Children – put away that beer immediately!' Mum comes tottering out of the house, all dolled up. In white jeans, a long turquoise shirt and pink pumps, she looks stunning.

I laugh and roll my eyes. 'You were drunk every weekend when you were only thirteen.'

'Unfortunately, I can't remember that.' She kisses me on the forehead. 'Don't set the house on fire while I'm away. Your father would throw me out.'

'Ha-ha-ha, very funny, Mum,' I call after her.

It's September. School is starting up again tomorrow. Mike, Vanessa, Stephen and I are planning to enjoy the last day and are barbecuing in the garden.

The summer holidays were great. I spent a lot of time with Stephen. But I got to know Mike too. He's really nice, and I'm happy for Vanessa.

'We're all set, then,' yells Vanessa.

I look at her. 'As if we couldn't do as we please with Mum here. She's totally laid back, as long as I don't come home high as a kite or get into trouble with the police.'

'That's because we do so much illegal stuff and we're constantly being hunted by the police.' Mike pulls Vanessa to him and kisses her.

'Well, I don't, but I'm not so sure about you.'

They are so sweet together. Mike adores Vanessa, and it does Vanessa good to have Mike. She's been much better since he's been around.

Stephen is standing happily at the barbecue, turning sausages and chicken thighs. Mike jumps up to help him. As if it were difficult to grill a bit of meat.

'So, have you a good resolution for the school year?' Vanessa is giving us all a challenging look.

Mike puts the first plate of grilled meat on the table. 'To drive my biology teacher mad,' he says.

'To find out why there's a fork stuck in the ceiling of the physics room. Little Red Riding Hood?'

I don't react to that name any more. My super-darling boyfriend named me that after I re-dyed my hair. It's even brighter than it was. Nobody would have believed it possible.

'Come on, honey.' Stephen leans across the table and gives me a quick kiss. 'It's a nice name.'

'For sure,' I murmur and answer, 'To do better than an E in Latin.'

'You'll never do that,' mutters Vanessa, her mouth full.

'You think not? And what are you going to do?'

'To do as well as last year.' She gives me a challenging look.

Stephen laughs, and I say, 'Show-off!' At the same moment, Mike says, 'Swot!'

Vanessa tosses her head playfully. 'You're all just jealous,' she says.

This is how my life has been since then. The life of a perfectly normal young person. Evenings with my best friends, now and again a party, romantic evenings for two.

I'm not saying that everything is perfect. It isn't. It's

flawed. Which means it's human. It's OK. Nice, in its own way.

There are moments in which sadness spills over and I have a cry about Toby and Joanne and the others who died that day. But then I pull myself together again and I realise how much good stuff there is in life.

Sometimes I can't get up in the morning because everything seems so sad. But then there's always someone – Mum, Dad, Stephen, Vanessa – who drags me out of bed and into life.

It feels good to breathe properly again. What happened, happened. I can't change it. And there's no guarantee that something like that will never happen again. Or even something worse. But one can't spend one's whole life in fear.

'What are you thinking about?' asks Stephen and strokes my hair.

'That it was a really lovely day.' It's lovely to be able to say something like that to him. You can see in his eyes how much he enjoys hearing that.

'Was?' Stephen grins and pulls me close.

I put a hand to his cheek and look into his eyes. I lean forward until my lips touch his. There it is again, that soft tickling feeling, those little explosions when my skin brushes his, as it used to be in my previous life. My heart beats against my ribs and I can almost touch my happiness. Stephen strokes my hair and my neck and this soft touch is enough to thrill me.

'Are you cold?' Stephen asks, concerned.

I shake my head. 'No,' I breathe. I can hardly wait for Mike and Vanessa to go, leaving me and Stephen alone.

For the moment, it's enough to sit in his lap. I hide my head in his shoulder and breathe in his smell. I feel very secure. Even though I know he can't protect me from everything. For the moment, that's enough.

I'm at the cemetery again. In my hand I have three bunches of flowers: one for Toby, one for Joanne and one for someone else.

I sidle along between the rows of graves. I'm not in a hurry. I stop in front of a black gravestone. I examine every detail carefully. The flowers, the inscription. He has relatives too, who miss him. And I can just imagine that it is even worse for them than it is for us.

I bend down slowly and finger the name: *Mathias Staudt*.

'We didn't know what we were doing to you. We never really thought about it. I'm very, very sorry.'

I look up at the sky, where a few clouds are gliding slowly along. The sun shines out strongly between them. The autumn is setting in. The autumn will turn to winter, the winter to spring and the spring to summer and the summer back to autumn again.

As the bell rings for the end of the ninth period this afternoon, I come barrelling, relieved, out of the school. Two junior pupils are running, laughing, towards the school bus. Mathias Staudt is battling with his bicycle lock, which seems to be stuck. My conscience starts to bother me, but I am also angry with myself for blaming myself about Mathias, of all people.

For a moment, I consider just sticking my nose in the air and flouncing off. But I go slowly towards him. He doesn't see me because he's standing with his back to me.

'Hi,' I say carefully. There's no reaction, so I say, 'Mathias?'

He turns around, confused. He's obviously not used to being spoken to. His eyes open wide in surprise as he recognises me.

'I just wanted to apologise for yesterday. I was a stupid cow. I'm really sorry.'

He gives me a sceptical look. He must think it's some sort of a joke.

'And don't take it so hard when Toby and his mates put you down. They just do it to make them feel cool. Typical boys.' I give him a wink. 'So, see you tomorrow.'

I can feel Mathias's amazed look on me as I turn my back on the school and go to my bus-stop.

So easy. It would have been so easy to say something nice to him. But in reality, this moment never happened. In reality I did flounce off.

Our behaviour was not right. And for that reason I am going to try every morning not to hate Mathias Staudt quite as much as the day before.

But nobody has the right to take away your life like that. Nobody has the right to take from mothers and fathers, sisters and brothers, grandmothers and grandfathers and friends what is most important to them.

Life is a brief and fragile thing. We only get one life. Everyone is special. And by killing someone, you don't just destroy one person but a whole world. That's why nobody has the right to point a gun at you. Ever.

Well, here we are. We're at the security checkpoint. Mum has packed her few things. The suitcases are beside her.

Mum is leaving. Here and now I have to say goodbye to a time that was terrible at first, but in the end was lovely. I hug her hard.

'Thanks for being there.' I sniff and suppress tears.

Mum takes my head in her hands. 'Don't cry. We're not saying goodbye for ever. Just for a while.'

'You're nearly crying yourself,' I whisper, not wanting to let her go. She helped me so much. She was so very much there again. But the most important thing is that I have a mum again. Even if I have tried to persuade myself that she's just a friend, she really is my mother.

Passengers pass me with their cases. Families. Singles. Business people. Officials. A little girl is crying because her father is leaving. She yells angrily, clings to him and throws herself on the floor.

I used to behave exactly like that when Dad had to go on business trips. And Mum just watched him go and envied him that he was able to travel.

I understand why she has to go. The world is calling her, ordering her to go to all those places where she hasn't been yet. That is what makes her happy. And everyone has to do what makes them happy. There's no use doing things for family, friends or whoever, if it only makes you unhappy. At the end of the day, we can't live for other people. We have to think of ourselves too.

'I'll send you postcards, OK? And emails. And at Christmas, I'll be back.'

I kiss her forehead. 'Don't make me any promises. You don't even know yourself when we'll see each other again. But that's OK.'

We hug one last time and then her flight is called. Very slowly, she lets go of my hand. And then she disappears through the departure gate.

She's like the wind. She comes when it blows her to me. I stand for a moment, looking after her, even after she's long gone. Then I turn and go. Believe it or not, I'm smiling a little. Not a lot, just a tiny bit.

It all starts with me sleeping in. If my boyfriend hadn't texted me, I'd have been late for school.

But as it turns out, I made it to school on time. Which is why I was there when it happened.

I wish now that I'd been anywhere else, as far away as humanly possible. And to think I used to be of the opinion that Latin homework was the worst thing in the world!

Then everything changed.